I0772040

DEADLY
SANCTUARY

SHANNON HOLLINGER

Published By Scene Of The Crime Publishing in 2025

ISBN: 979-8-9895116-3-1

No AI was used in the production of this work.

To all the readers out there who have become friends. I couldn't have made this transition without your support.

CHAPTER 1

It should have been me. I'm the one who should be lying in the box at the front of the room right now. And it's clear that everyone knows it.

Dr. Parsons, the Bureau shrink, tracks my every movement like I'm a grenade missing its pin. My boss, Assistant Director in Charge Jacobson, shoots wary glances in my direction with increasing frequency the closer I get to where she sits in the front row beside the bereaved spouse, my once closest friend who can't even stomach the sight of me anymore. Even the undertaker, who doesn't know who I am or the role I played in our reason for being here today, is staring at me.

The line in front of me moves. The queue behind me surges forward, forcing me to take a step closer to the casket. It's a step I'm not ready to take.

My knees lock in an attempt to stay upright as the rest of me threatens to buckle. A flood of heat spreads beneath my flesh, forcing a tidal wave of sweat to the surface of my skin. I draw deep breaths, fighting against the dizziness that's threatening to pull me under the dark shroud of unconsciousness.

Not that loss of consciousness doesn't have its allure right now. But while it might be the right time, it's certainly not the right place. And let's face it—while the old me might have had the uncanny ability to fall asleep anywhere, a fact many of my former teachers can attest to—the new me can't even relax when anyone else is in the same room.

The mourners ahead shift, revealing a flash of polished wood. I tell myself to look away, but I can't, my gaze inexplicably locked on the bright white satin lining. To the startling sight of a pair of hands folded together across a dark suit. No one told me it would be an open casket.

I don't think I can do this.

I glance around, looking for an escape route, but the crowd is too thick. There are too many people in here, the air stifling and stale, and though I know it can't be possible, that I must be imagining it, tinged with the scent of death. Only, I don't have to imagine it, do I?

Because the stench had been overwhelming in that damp basement carved out of the earth, dirt walls stained dark with the blood of the women who had found themselves trapped down there before me. I may have fought my way out, but a part of me never left.

Every time I close my eyes, I find myself back there: Hands cuffed together around the frigid metal pole behind me. Heart tattooing the walls of my chest with terror. A battle I had no hope of winning.

And yet, here I am.

Alive, while my partner begins the process of decay in a shiny wooden box he would have hated in a room filled with people he didn't like. He wasn't an easy man to get along with. Even those who loved him would have to agree.

But I was not one of those people. Somehow, that makes it worse.

I gasp for air, but my lungs won't work right, refusing to inhale as I suddenly find myself at the head of the line. I know I'm staring down at his face, but that's not what I see. It doesn't matter if my eyes are open or closed. His memory will forever be intertwined with what was done to him, the way he appeared the last time I saw him.

Does anyone else here know the horrors concealed beneath the suit he wears?

I feel an arm around my back, pulling me away, fingers trying to loosen my grip on the casket, but all I can see are the wounds that took this man's life.

We didn't get along. To be more precise, we couldn't stand each other. He'd made my life miserable for the last year. But I never would have wished this on him. He shouldn't be the one who ended up dead.

In my mind, I picture his face as it was in life. His eyes open, flashing with accusation. His lips curl. His voice drips with venom as he tells me it's all my fault. That I'm too rash. Too emotional.

But the old me never cared what he thought. She would have left here today and gone on to live her best life just to spite the bully. She might have even leaned down and given him a kiss on the forehead just to see if he'd roll over in his grave. But the stranger who's been left in her place can't function well enough to do either.

My pulse thunders in my ears as I allow myself to be led away. Pushed down into a chair. Someone removes my jacket and wraps my trembling hands around a cup of water. My dry throat feels like it sizzles as I take a small sip. Before I know it, I've drained the whole glass.

But I'm still overheating.

Because the guilt and the shame and the regret that I'm buried under are too much. Too heavy. I feel like a hypocrite for being here. For trying to mourn a man I'd wished out of my life so many times before. Just not like this.

Slowly, I get myself in hand, my surroundings breaking through the fog. The shrink sits by my side while Director Jacobson hovers above me, the two exchanging a look that lets me know I won't be returning to work any time soon. Not that a quick return was in the forecast before this meltdown, but I can tell that eventually just changed to possibly.

Years of hard work, an entire career spent striving to reach what I'd only recently started to attain, all gone in an instant, another causality of that horrible decision I made. When will the repercussions end? What else will I lose?

I don't have much left.

Just my guilt and that incessant buzzing that won't stop. The noise pauses for a moment, proving me wrong, then starts again. With an exasperated sigh Director Jacobson pats down my jacket, removes my cell from the pocket, and lifts it to her ear.

"Special Agent Cassidy Knox's phone."

Her expression falters as she listens to whoever's speaking on the other end of the line. Her voice is uncharacteristically gentle as she holds the phone toward me, telling me I need to take the call. I can only imagine what fresh catastrophe life has in store for me now.

And just like that, the bottom drops out.

There's nothing like being at one funeral when you get a call that you're needed at another. It's certainly not the type of in demand that anyone wants to be.

Make that nothing. I have absolutely nothing left.

CHAPTER 2

The miles pass by in a blur, a steady stream of asphalt disappearing beneath my tires entirely too quickly, the fifteen-plus hour drive between my apartment in Virginia and my hometown of Gator Glade in Florida ticking away too fast. Once again, I've made a huge mistake. I'd thought there was plenty of time. But I was wrong.

The realization has left me almost as numb as the loss of the one person I had left in this world—the only person in my life who would be glad it wasn't me inside that casket back in Virginia. I'm now officially alone. There's no one left to care.

My grandfather had sacrificed everything for me, had pulled himself together when his own heart was broken, taken me in and raised me after the death of my parents. And how had I repaid him? The moment I got the chance, I left.

Not only that—I never went back to visit, not even once in the last twenty years.

Now, as I tell myself for the hundredth time that I'm never going to see him again, trying to get reality to set in, I feel… empty. Hollowed out by grief and loss.

The steady drone of rubber on road is the perfect soundtrack for this particular trip, the radio long since turned off, the music drowned out by the loudness of my thoughts. Because I still can't believe he's gone.

What's the house going to feel like without him there? Who's taking care of the animals? What am I going to do?

I have a life, a home, a career over a thousand miles away. Or, at least, I did. Now I'm not sure what I have.

Director Jacobson's voice fills my mind, accompanied by the sympathetic smile she'd given me as she said, "Take it easy on yourself, Agent Knox. No one expects you to bounce back overnight. These things take time to work through."

By *things*, I knew she meant the panic attacks that followed me out of that basement. I'd always been so calm before. So steady.

"Get some rest. We'll talk again when you're feeling better."

She said it like she was confident that day would come, even though I suspect she wasn't. That makes two of us.

I know it's normal practice for an agent to be put on administrative leave after taking a life in the line of duty, but there'd been no end date on the paperwork I was given. No stipulations for what I needed to complete in order to return. No assurances that my job would still be there once I dealt with the nightmares that plague me.

What if they never go away, if they're part of my new normal?

I swallow hard as I notice that the landscape has changed outside my window, the number of alligators sunning themselves along the bank of the canal to my right increasing. I'm almost home, and I'm terrified of pulling into that bumpy dirt driveway without a solid plan in place to make sure that I drive back out. But I can't think that clearly.

Already, the claustrophobia of the small town I

left behind is closing in on me as a long-buried memory of Matt's face resurfaces. My grandfather would have told me if he'd left. Or if his father, Sheriff Kingston, had retired. Which means that all my old problems are still waiting for me. And my new problems aren't willing to step aside and wait their turn.

My anxiety grows as I pass the Indian village. My heart races as I drive by the roadside café. And as the battered, faded black mailbox on the sun-bleached red post comes into view, my hands begin to shake.

I tighten my fingers on the steering wheel, trying to still the trembling, but it grows worse as I turn off the road. Each dip of the pitted drive is an assault, my body too rigid to cushion the blows as my vehicle bounces and sways.

The thicket of palmettos and pines that pen me in open up revealing a barn straight ahead, a series of outbuildings and paddocks to my right, and to my left, like an oasis in a desert, my eyes blinking repeatedly as if to make sure it's truly there, the ranch-style house where I spent most of my youth.

The numbness burns off as if scorched by a blowtorch, the dam that's held my tears at bay finally collapsing, releasing a torrent of emotion. I'm hurt and I'm scared. Everything I've spent my adult life working for is on the line. And the one person I can talk to about it is gone and never coming back.

Pulling up in front of the house, I put my car in park and turn off the engine. But I don't have the energy to get out. The heat quickly builds inside the vehicle, a thick coat of sweat slicking my skin, my blood, thickened after two decades spent in a cold climate, simmering.

It's a fitting ending. One I deserve. I lean my forehead against the steering wheel, my head throbbing, my lungs struggling to draw in the thick, sizzling air, my brain feeling like it's three sizes too big for my skull and beginning to boil, when… *tap, tap, tap.*

I hold my breath, stifled sobs shaking my body as I listen. *Tap, tap, tap.* The noise comes again.

Lifting my head, I gaze at my tear blurred surroundings, a flash of motion outside my window drawing my attention. Fisting my eyes dry, I blink in confusion. Then burst out laughing.

The sound of it is strained and hysterical and accompanied by the soundtrack of the pygmy goat *baaing* as it once again knocks its tiny hoof against the glass. Unbuckling my seatbelt, I crack the door open. Fresh air rushes inside, carrying with it the scents of my childhood—sweet grass, hay, manure, the swamp.

"What are you doing out here, huh?" I ask, rubbing the coarse hair on the goat's knobby head.

Suddenly, my worries about who's been taking care of the animals since my grandfather's death come rushing back, and my personal problems seem insignificant. His rescues were his family, just as much as I was, maybe even more so. They might be hungry, thirsty, in need. Even a day without water can be deadly in a climate like this.

I exit the vehicle, muscles stiff and tight. My bladder begs for release after the long journey. My skin craves air conditioning, my parched throat a drink. But my own needs are going to have to wait.

"Let's go see what kind of a mess we have on our hands, shall we?"

The goat sounds his reply, leading the way to the barn in that frisking gait they have, kicking up his heels every time he stops to check that I'm behind him. A mule lifts its head from the grass it's grazing on, watching as I pass. A pelican with half a wing missing flops down from its perch on a fence post and waddles after me.

Growing up in Gator Glade wasn't easy. The town is tiny, with distinct lines drawn between those born to the paved streets and those of us born in the swamp. Money's scarce, with opportunity even scarcer. It's a hard way of life.

Yet despite all its faults, the Glade has one thing that no place else has. Stepping into the shade of the barn I draw a deep breath, the anxiety that's been constricting my chest finally easing for the first time in longer than I can remember, even before what happened. Tension melts off me with each step.

A cow lows as I pass its stall, gazing at me with wide brown eyes. A pair of pigs oink, their little corkscrew tails twitching happily as they root their snouts into a fresh bucket of slop. There's a strange noise coming from the next stall, one I can't immediately place.

As I crane my neck curiously, quickening my step to see what's inside, I catch a glimpse of motion from the corner of my eye. My breath catches. My skin tightens. My brain screams danger. I look around frantically, searching for an escape route, but I'm trapped as the shadow approaches, quick and large and most definitely human.

CHAPTER 3

I spin to face the intruder, hands raised and curled into fists like I'm prepared to defend myself, but it's a lie. My entire body is trembling. I can't catch my breath. My heart beats against the walls of my chest so violently I feel injured, dizzy, somehow simultaneously too hot and too cold.

"Whoa, hey!" Darkness gathers around the edges of my vision, making it narrow. I blink, trying to clear the gray spots so I can see more than just a pair of palms held up toward me as if to ward off an attack. "I'm sorry. I didn't mean to startle you. I didn't know anyone else was here."

Noticing the half bale of hay he'd been carrying, now on the ground at his feet, I realize he couldn't see me. The old me would apologize. The new me can't speak. I'm still struggling too hard to draw air.

"I, uh, don't know if you remember me. Jake Walker?"

Of course I remember Jake. Most of my earliest memories include him. He'd been my first love. Well, at the very least, I'd been enamored by him in the way that four-year-old girls fall for seven-year-old boys who treat them with patience and kindness.

Then life intervened. Our playdates ended when my parents died and his mom took off. But I never forgot him, and a decade later when I reached high school, he'd been my first real crush. Not that he'd known I was alive by then.

But he does now, and for all the wrong reasons as my body betrays me by continuing to have a meltdown despite the lack of danger. Humiliated, I pray that it's not really him, but as I raise my gaze and my vision clears, I see his familiar features. Dark, unruly hair. Full lips. A strong jaw.

Only, now that jaw is heavily stubbled. His tall frame has filled out, shoulders broad and muscular. It is him. Except now the boy's a man. I swallow hard as I note the changes.

"Are you all right?"

"I'm fine," I pant. And then, trying to convince myself, I say it again. "I'm fine."

"Maybe you should sit. Let's get you—"

But there's no time for him to help me anywhere because I'm already taking his suggestion, my back sliding painfully down the wood slats of the stall behind me, the scabs covering the wound between my shoulder blades tugging sharply before an edge rips free with a burst of searing pain.

Jake curses, eyes wide, a look of horror etched across his face as I land in the dirt.

"It's okay," he says, though judging by the way his voice shakes as he kneels next to me, he's not sure that it is. "Just breathe."

I resist the urge to roll my eyes. It's not like I'm not trying.

"Sorry. That was a stupid thing to say."

He gives me a tense smile, then sits beside me. It's a relief to have his gaze off me, to no longer be watched as I'm caught in the throes of panic.

His shoulder nudges against mine as he says, "I

knew this little girl once, a long time ago. Had the same golden hair that you do. She was absolutely fearless. She didn't care about getting hurt or in trouble. Once she made up her mind to do something, there was no changing it."

I remember being that girl. I miss her.

"One day, this girl was on the playground. On the swing set."

My stomach tightens as I realize what story he's going to tell.

"She took that swing as high as it could go. Higher than I'd ever seen anyone take it before. But that wasn't enough for her. Because right as she reached the top, she let go of the chain, threw her arms wide, and jumped."

I'll never forget that weightless feeling as I flew through the air. Or how it felt when I landed flat on my back, the breath knocked from my lungs so hard I thought I'd never be able to fill them again. Kind of like now.

In that moment, I hadn't known what was happening. I was terrified. A part of me thought I was dying.

As I laid there gasping for breath, it had been Jake who ran over and knelt beside me in the dirt. Who took my hand and told me I'd be okay. And just like that, I wasn't scared anymore. Because I'd believed him.

"Man, she hit hard. I think we were both scared that she was really hurt. But in the end, she was okay."

I shake my head.

"She's not?" he asks, voice tense.

"She's still bruised," I choke out. It's the truth, in more ways than he'll ever know.

Jake chuckles. "Stay here, I'll be right back."

Like me going somewhere is an actual possibility

right now, no matter how badly I wish I could crawl away and hide. I cup my hands over my nose and mouth, trying to get my breathing under control. I'm beyond embarrassed. I'm positively mortified.

I think how differently this would have gone just a few weeks ago. Long to return to being the woman I used to be. But is that even possible? Or did that version of myself die in that basement? Am I going to be this broken, skittish, terrified wreck forever?

Jake returns from the tack room with a paper cup of water. Squatting beside me, he offers me the drink. "Here."

I take it from him with trembling hands, pretending not to notice the concern in his eyes as I take small sips, forcing them past the lump in my throat.

"There you go," he says encouragingly.

My cheeks feel like they're on fire. Here I am, completely losing it in front of the one person from my past whose opinion of me still matters.

"I see you've met Stephano."

I glance around, peering into the darkened corners of the barn, but I don't see anyone. Just the goat, now butting his head gently against Jake's knee.

"He's a little escape artist."

The tightness in my chest eases enough for me to ask, "The goat's name is Stephano?"

Jake gives me the lopsided grin I remember so well from my youth, the one that made my knees go weak and butterflies dance in my stomach.

"We tried to rename him, but he won't answer to anything else." He reaches out, stopping the goat from climbing onto my lap. "So Stephano it is."

His fingers brush mine as he takes the now empty cup from me and stands. I'm left staring at my hand, still tingling from his touch. It's the first non-negative sensation my body's experienced since I woke up on a hard dirt floor, cuffed to a metal support beam.

My chest loosens. My lungs fill. My body stills.

Jake raises his voice so I can hear him as he returns to the tack room. "With the way this guy jumps, it's impossible to keep him contained unless he's completely caged in. Luckily, he heads straight for the nearest human when he escapes. So don't be surprised if you find him waiting for you on the doorstep when you get up in the morning."

He reappears and hands me the cup back.

I thank him, then quickly look away. Now that I can breathe again and the trembling's stopped, now that everything has calmed except my pulse, I'm painfully aware of how awful I must look. And how Jake has somehow grown even better looking over the years.

But none of that matters. Or, at least, it shouldn't. It's not like I'm moving back. I'm only here for however long it takes to plan my grandfather's funeral and figure out what I'm going to do with the sanctuary. I owe it to him to make sure that all the animals he worked so hard to protect find good homes.

Little Stephano and the pigs and…

"Is that a zebra?"

I scramble to my feet, not believing my eyes.

"Yeah. A pregnant zebra."

I raise my eyebrows and give him a look, all the reasons I had for feeling so awkward suddenly forgotten. I might have been gone for a while, but there's no need to state the obvious. "A *very* pregnant zebra. When was the last time the vet was here?"

"Two days ago. He's kind of lost his patience with me. Said not to call him out again until she's ready to foal."

"Is she friendly?"

"Very."

I offer my hand for her to sniff, then slide the bolt on the door and back my way inside. She steps away, allowing me entry. I let her take her time inspecting me, her soft muzzle brushing against me as she checks my scent. Her upper lip lifts, giving me a look at her teeth. I'm shocked by what I see.

"The vet's giving you a hard time for being concerned about a mare this old giving birth?"

"Yes."

"Jerk," I mutter. "What's her name?"

"Daisy."

"Hey, Daisy," I say, softening my voice. "Hey, girl." I scratch behind her ear, then let my hand travel down her neck, keeping my palm pressed firmly against her as I reach the bulge of her stomach. "That's a good girl."

I give her a pat, then exit the stall.

"The foal's dropped. Has she been acting restless at all?"

"Not really."

"Lying down?"

"No."

"Hmm. Then the birth's probably still a few days out."

"That's what the vet said. But if it's okay with you, I'd still like to camp out here at night, just to keep an eye on her."

For the first time, I notice the tent off to the side of the aisle.

"You've been staying here at night?"

"Yeah. I hope that's okay."

"It's fine. It's just… it can't be very comfortable."

This time he's the one who looks away, rubbing

the back of his neck as he shrugs. "I don't mind. She meant a lot to…" A lump grows in my throat as he hesitates. Then, "Listen, Cassidy. I'm really sorry about Butch. He was a great guy. One of the best."

I nod, swallowing hard.

"You've been helping him out?"

"Yeah."

"For how long?"

"Since you left."

I flinch. Surely if he'd been helping Butch out for twenty years, my grandfather would have mentioned him.

But maybe he had. Even if he'd said the name, I wouldn't have made the connection. Wouldn't have thought he was talking about my Jake. Not my, geez, I've been back in the swamp for less than an hour and already the heat is baking my brain.

"You work for him, then?"

"No. I have a day job, I'm just here as much as I can be."

"Why?"

He gives me a funny look, like I should know the answer. But I don't, so I stare at him until he says, "I owe him a lot. He… Butch helped me when everyone else thought the effort was a waste."

It rings true. Butch was the savior of lost souls, both animal and human. And Jake, well, let's be honest. He'd been trouble long before I left town. Sherriff Kingston had a personal vendetta against him, pulled him in whenever he saw the chance, even if the charges rarely stuck.

Jake clears his throat, like he knows what I'm thinking. But when I look at him, his eyes are void of the discomfort you'd expect if you knew someone was thinking about your criminal past. They're filled with sympathy, instead.

"What happened earlier… your panic attack?"

I want to look away, but I can't. It's like I'm an insect under glass and his gaze has me pinned in place.

"Is that because of, I mean, I know his loss must have been a shock. Or did something else happen?"

"Like what?" I ask, voice harsh.

"Butch was real proud about your career, but he worried."

My jaw clenches, the ridge that's formed on the inside of my right cheek pinched painfully between my teeth. Butch didn't tell people what I did for a living. Not unless he really trusted them. Which means that Jake was either part of my grandfather's inner circle—or he's lying.

"He was concerned about how dangerous your new position might turn out to be."

Butch had raised the same concern with me. And he'd been right, hadn't he? He always was. It was like he had some kind of sixth sense, an uncanny ability to predict the future and even though I knew that, I hadn't listened.

But for the first time, when I think about what happened, I don't find myself sucked into a vortex of panic. Is it being home, or something else? Maybe some*one* else?

I'm being ridiculous. Chances are I'm just too worn out to get worked up again so soon.

And though I can't deny that Jake's presence seems to have a calming effect on me, that's because I'm remembering the boy I once knew. The man he is now is a stranger. One I'm not sure I should trust.

Just because he makes me feel more relaxed than the Bureau shrink that I—my eyes find the clock high on the wall beside the door to the tack room. Shoot. I'm late.

"If there's something you need? Anything that I can do to help…"

"I've got to go."

Jake's expression crumples. "I'm sorry if I overstepped—"

"No, it's not that. We'll talk later, okay?" I offer, hurrying down the aisle back toward the bright light of day.

"Is it okay if I camp out, then?"

"Of course. Come up to the house if you get hungry or need anything. I just, there's a call I've got to make."

I don't wait for a reply, jogging out into the sunshine and across the yard before I can think twice about the conversation that just took place. Because it already feels like my head's been done in. And as I pause at my car, grabbing my bags before heading inside, I know it's only going to get worse the longer I'm here.

CHAPTER 4

I turn the handle and the door pushes open, just like I knew it would. Butch never bothered with locks. He had his reasons. And as I cast a glance toward the barn before lowering my hand from the deadbolt without turning it, I'm surprised to discover that I have mine.

Dumping my bags on the floor, I pull my phone from my pocket, finding that I've already missed several calls. Cursing, I press the button to return them. Ringing fills my ear as I cross the darkened room, leaving the lights off, and drop onto the couch.

"Hello?"

"I'm sorry I missed your calls. I was running late."

"Anything I need to know about?"

I make a face, rolling my eyes. Draw a deep breath and release it, forcing a pleasantness I don't feel into my tone as I say, "No. Unless you want to hear about an escaped goat named Stephano?"

"That won't be necessary." I didn't think it would. This guy only wants to hear about doom and gloom and the things I imagine going bump in the night. As if on cue, he asks, "How have the panic attacks been?"

"Fine."

"Fine?"

"Yes."

"Which means?"

"That there haven't been any."

"Really?" The way he says the word lets me know that he finds the statement hard to believe. But it's true.

Unless you count what just happened in the barn, which I don't. Or the twenty minutes I spent in a fast-food parking lot shaking uncontrollably because I mistook a crow taking flight as someone coming after me. Or the slight delay to my travel plans when I couldn't bring myself to exit a bathroom stall because I thought I heard someone else breathing in the restroom with me, even though I couldn't see any feet below the partition wall.

"That's excellent, Cassidy."

But he sounds disappointed.

"Maybe this trip home will prove to be a good thing. I took the liberty of finding someone for you to talk to down there. So you can continue your therapy."

"That's okay."

"I'm afraid it isn't up for debate. Not if you want to continue on with the agency."

My throat grows so tight it makes the insides of my ears itch. I dig the nails of my free hand deep into the couch cushion beside me. It takes every ounce of strength I have to regulate my voice as I say, "I see."

"This isn't a new development, Agent Knox. You knew the terms of your treatment. Nothing's changed."

Except maybe something has.

I don't know how to explain it, not to Dr. Parsons or myself. It's not something I understand, and I don't want to risk saying something that might jeopardize my future until I do. All I know is that when I left the city, I could barely breathe.

But here, on this land my grandfather took so much pride in? Inside this house? It's gotten a bit easier.

"I've taken the liberty of making some appointments for you. The first is tomorrow at one o'clock."

Anger flares beneath my skin. Strangely enough, it feels good. I've been so scared of everyone and everything, it's nice to know that I'm still capable of other emotions.

"I wish you hadn't done that."

"Agent Knox—"

"No. I understand that the Bureau requires me to undergo counseling. But the circumstances have changed. I'm not just sitting around my apartment waiting for the next hoop you give me to jump through. And I'm not on vacation, either."

I glare around the room, barely able to make out my surroundings in the gloom, but I don't need to see to know what's there. The edge of the coffee table in front of me is scuffed from decades of shoes propped on it. The surface is stained by markers, nail polish, shellac, and an Olympics of water rings.

That hump among the shadows across from me is Butch's favorite chair. There will be a stack of books beside it on the left, an old stump with a thimble, a chunk of wood, and a whittling knife on top on the right.

I know that there will be a dish with butter half melted from the heat on the kitchen table. A tower of towels and blankets in the laundry room. More animal food than people food in the pantry, along with enough medical supplies to run a small clinic. And something about knowing all these things about this place that I occupy gives me a confidence that I've been lacking in my interactions with this man.

"I'm here on bereavement. I have a funeral to

plan, an animal sanctuary to run, and an estate to sort out."

"I understand that."

"Do you?"

"I assure you I do."

"Then what made you think it would be a good idea to schedule appointments on my behalf when you have no idea—when *I* have no idea—what my days are going to look like yet? Do you really think I can just drop everything and drive to—where's the office located?"

"Naples."

"To drive over a half hour each way to Naples? Tomorrow? When I haven't even been down here for twenty-four hours yet?"

When he doesn't respond, I say, "Please forward me the contact information and let their office know that I'll be in touch to make my own appointments. My paperwork requires four sessions a month. This is my second this week, so I have plenty of time to get things sorted, don't I?"

"You need to speak with someone more often than that."

"I'm not sure that I do."

"I'm afraid I'm going to have to make note of your refusal to take my recommendations."

Though the threat remains unspoken, it's there. The Bureau likes its agents to follow orders. Pushing back on this is equivalent to jeopardizing my career.

I take a moment to let the possible ramifications sink in. The entire fifteen-plus hour drive down here, I thought that my job was all I had left. Losing what I'd spent my entire adult life working so hard for seemed like the worst thing that could happen to me that hadn't already occurred.

But being at the sanctuary has reminded me of

something important that I somehow forgot. Butch might not be here anymore, but the home he created for us still is. And the woman he raised me to be is still inside me somewhere. I wouldn't be here right now if she wasn't.

Because he raised me to be a fighter. That's what I am. What I've done. First for my life, and now, well, I guess the battle that lies ahead of me is for my future. And I intend to find the old me and make my grandfather proud.

CHAPTER 5

Jake never came up to the house last night. I can't help feeling a bit disappointed. I have so many questions, and I feel like he might hold some of the answers. But after the abrupt way I left things yesterday, I can't help feeling like I messed things up already.

I'm good at that. And I know I probably should have gone back out to the barn to smooth things over, but I didn't feel fit for human company after my conversation with Dr. Parsons. A residual anger simmered deep inside me long after the call had ended and it felt… good.

It was a welcome change from the constant fear that's stalked me, lurking over my shoulder, seizing every opportunity to wrap me in its tight embrace. For the first time since I left that basement, I felt like I had some power over what happened to me. Like I had the courage to face the challenges that lie ahead.

So, I kept that fire stoked, using it to burn through the grief that fogged my brain while I made a list of all the difficult tasks that await me. Because I don't even know where Butch's body is. I was so shocked when I received the news that it didn't even occur to me to ask.

But that's just the first thing on my list. Because there's a whole funeral to plan, and the truth is, I have no idea what Butch would want. Burial or cremation? Open casket or closed? Reception or not? It's not something we ever discussed.

I stood staring into his closet late into the night, wondering which of the rarely worn dress clothes hanging inside he'd hate to wear the least. Or should I choose what he was most comfortable in—a pair of well-worn jeans and a T-shirt—for his funeral attire?

Now, glancing at the outfit I'd settled on where it lies draped over the back of the couch, I wonder if I made the right decision. I tell myself not to second-guess it. Chances are that none of this would matter to Butch. I can't help but let it matter to me, though. Because once all these decisions are made, that's it. He'll really be gone.

And I'm not ready to let him go just yet.

I blink against the tears invading my eyes, trying to muster up some of my anger from last night to steel myself with, but there's none left. The coals have cooled, leaving me full of doubt and regret.

I do my best to ignore the anxiety building within me as I hurry into the kitchen to make a pot of coffee. I don't want things to be awkward between Jake and me. As much as I hate to admit it, I'm going to need his help. I have no idea how many animals are here right now, which ones are being rehabbed, the state of their health, or even their diets.

Of all the questions I have swirling around my head about what Butch would want, there's only one answer I know with absolute certainty—his main concern would be that every animal under his care receive the absolute best treatment. So that's what I'm going to make my priority.

I yawn as I press the brew button, wishing I was still in bed after the late night I had. But I'd set my alarm extra early to make sure I caught Jake before he left. I've pulled two mugs from a cabinet and am debating how to bring out cream and sugar to the barn in case Jake wants some for his coffee when I hear the growl of an engine fire up.

Rushing to the window, I watch as a black truck pulls out from behind the barn, trundling slowly down the pitted driveway in a cloud of dust until it disappears. I'm too late. Despite the early hour, he's already gone. He was probably hoping to avoid me. And who can blame him?

I look at the pot of coffee like it somehow betrayed me. It's still too early to start making phone calls, but the idea of sitting around alone with my thoughts is unbearable. So I head outside instead.

I walk over to the paddock where a cow grazes, ignoring my arrival. There's a large fatty tumor bulging from the side of her neck. It's most likely benign, but these types of growths can be problematic, especially when they're located in an area where the animal can scratch. There's a fading scab and a fresh layer of balm on the lump to confirm this.

Jake must have applied it before he left. I continue on, wondering what else he did.

Stepping into the shelter of the barn feels like claiming sanctuary in a church. I pause for a moment on the threshold, allowing my eyes to adjust to the dim light inside. Listening to the sounds of the animals within.

Stephano frisks over to greet me, bumping his head playfully against my knee before bounding forward, looking over his shoulder to see if I'm following. He leads the way from one stall to the next like a tour guide. Or a good host introducing me to all his friends.

I'm largely ignored by the animals as they eat their breakfast. It adds to the sense of shame I feel that of all the animals here, these creatures who played such a big and important part of my grandfather's life, I know exactly two of their names. There was a time when I would have known everything about them, even the ones I'd never met.

When had he stopped telling me about his life? Or had I stopped listening? I called him every other week and yet, in this moment, I can't for the life of me recall any of the things we spoke about. Had he mentioned a zebra to me before? For that matter, had he mentioned Jake?

Even if he had, would I have made the connection? Probably not. I most likely would have assumed he was talking about some other Jake, not the one I used to play with as a little girl. The sweet kid who grew up into the bad boy I drooled over in high school.

All I know for sure is that somewhere along the way that boy became the one Butch depended on, and me? If Jake hadn't fed the animals this morning before he left, I'd be completely lost. I know I should feel grateful, but it's just more weight added to the burden on my back instead.

I stop following Stephano when we reach Daisy's stall. The mare glances up from her hay, then returns to eating. Her side stretches as the baby within shifts and I make the unborn foal a silent promise—I'll be here to help welcome it into the world.

Stephano circles back around to see what's taking me so long, interrupting my thoughts as he puts his hooves up onto the stall door, knocking into a plastic grocery bag tied to the latch, making it rustle. Frowning, I free the bag and open it, finding a notebook inside, my name written in all caps on the cover.

Flipping it open, I find an array of names, descriptions, backgrounds, dietary and medical information, a mini dossier for every animal here. On the one hand, it's a huge relief to have this information, but on the other, a crippling disappointment. Jake must have wanted to make sure I had everything I needed because he's not coming back.

I force a swallow past the lump in my throat as I skim the contents. Some I recognize, like Chomp, an alligator who'd lost the top half of its jaw to a hunting snare and came to call the fenced-in pond out back home almost thirty years ago. Others, like Flap, the pelican with a crippled wing that I'd seen when I first arrived yesterday, I'm learning about for the first time.

The notes are detailed, containing everything I need to take over their care. I'm grateful to Jake, even if he didn't want to stick around to help. I flip back to the first page.

Here's a bit to get you started. I'll be back tonight to answer any questions. I'll bring pizza, if you're interested. —J

Too many emotions run through me to identify just one. Though a part of me had hoped I'd get a chance to spend more time with Jake, if only to learn more about what Butch had been going through recently, it doesn't simplify things, does it? If anything, it feels like everything's just become much more complicated.

CHAPTER 6

Fake leather upholstery sticks to the backs of my thighs as I sit across the desk from the undertaker at Shady Groves Funeral Home. I shift my weight, the material pulling away from my skin like Cling Wrap as I frown at the man. He stares back at me with a blank expression.

"What do you mean, everything's been taken care of?"

It hadn't taken many calls this morning to find where Butch's body was. When the county medical examiner's office told me they didn't have him, I tried the morgue at the closest hospital, who informed me the body had already been identified and released to the funeral home. Still, I've been left with so many questions, and this man doesn't seem to want to help with any of them.

"Mr. Donovan's funeral plan—"

"What funeral plan?"

"The one he left with his estate lawyer."

Butch had an estate lawyer? None of this makes sense. I knew he'd had a will drawn up, but he'd done that ages ago, after I first came to live with him. He certainly hadn't had a funeral plan at that time, just a document naming me as his beneficiary, since there was no one else left. And the friend who'd written that document moved away before I did.

The man continues to stare at me with a complete lack of emotion, a direct opposite to the turmoil and confusion I'm feeling.

"And this plan laid out all the details for his funeral?"

"Correct."

"Including the clothes he wanted to wear for his burial?"

"Yes."

"Which have been brought to you already?"

"Yes."

"By who?"

Finally, his indifferent expression falters.

"I wasn't the one who accepted them, so I'm afraid I can't say."

"But you're sure you have the right guy?"

"Yes."

Had Butch somehow known he was going to die? Had he been sick and not told me?

"What was his cause of death?"

"I wasn't told."

"Who identified him?"

"I had nothing to do with that. The identification was made at the morgue."

It should be a relief to find that everything's been arranged already. Instead, it's a blow I don't feel strong enough to weather.

I had just turned five when my parents died and Butch took me in. The only details I remember about them are the things that Butch told me. He was my only family. And I was his.

I owed the man everything. And yet somehow, is it possible that I made him feel like I wouldn't even come back home to attend his funeral?

The thought fills my stomach with a dull ache,

because if I'm being honest with myself? Yeah, it's entirely possible. I've avoided this place like the plague. Forced him to find someone to take care of his animals and make a plane trip he hated to visit me instead. And when he'd canceled his trip a couple months ago, I hadn't thought twice about it.

I knew it was getting harder for him to travel, and yet it never crossed my mind that my opportunities to see him might be running out. He'd always been so strong and steady and dependable. Despite his age, the possibility of losing him hadn't occurred to me. I think a part of me believed he'd live forever.

Taking my silence for acceptance, the undertaker says, "We're planning to hold the funeral Saturday, if that works for you."

I grip the edge of the desk, trying to ground myself. "But that's tomorrow."

He nods with a patient smile, like I'm a child just learning the days of the week.

"Everything's ready to go on our end."

It's too soon. I'm not ready. And yet, what's there to gain by delaying the inevitable? Still, I try to think of an excuse to do so.

"But there's no time to notify everyone. He has friends who will want to attend."

His smile tightens as he says, "That's all been taken care of already. This is a small town, Ms. Knox. I'm sure those who haven't received a direct notification by now have heard through word of mouth. Don't worry. I'm sure plenty of your grandfather's loved ones will show up to pay their respects."

The fake leather beneath him squeaks as he leans forward to reach across the desk, laying his hand on mine. It takes all my willpower not to bare my teeth at him. A large part of me longs to tell him what happened to the last man who touched me.

But he's just trying to be kind. I know I should be grateful for the gesture, but I'm just not capable. Because everything's moving too fast.

I give him a nod as I pull away from the physical contact and stand. Turn to leave his office. I'm sure he can't wait to be rid of me, but he's going to have to wait a little longer, because a thought strikes on my way out the door. I stop on the threshold and face him.

"The funeral plan? Do you know which estate lawyer it came from?"

"Myers and Kleinman."

The rising lump in my throat has substance behind it. I think I might be sick. Because I've heard of Myers and Kleinman before. And they aren't estate planners.

I mumble a quick, "Thank you," before leaving, my jaw firmly clenched as I stumble from the funeral home into the blinding sunlight. Hurrying across the parking lot, I get in my vehicle and crank the engine. Lock the door and look around, checking to see if there's anyone else nearby before pulling out my phone.

A new question has just risen to the top of my list—why would a corporate law firm have Butch's funeral plan?

Unlocking my screen, I enter Myers and Kleinman in the search bar, hoping that I'm mistaken.

I'm not.

Not only that, but it's worse than I thought. A quick perusal of their website makes it clear—these guys aren't just corporate lawyers—they're corporate lawyers for clients who have a *lot* of money. Like, a lot, a lot. Which does not include my grandfather.

What had Butch gotten himself into?

CHAPTER 7

I rub my palm back and forth over my hip as I stare at the images of the ritzy law firm on my phone. It takes me a moment to realize what I'm looking for. My gun.

But it's not there.

I'm not entirely sure where it is, but I imagine it's probably in an evidence box somewhere in Virginia right now. The same for my backup piece. I'm not supposed to wear my service weapon while I'm on leave anyway—not until I've been cleared by a shrink. And let's face it, between the way our last conversation went and how my brain is feeling right now, that's probably not going to happen any time soon.

It hasn't bothered me until this moment. After seeing close up the damage a firearm wreaked on my partner, just the thought of holding one had turned my stomach. It's one thing to shoot a gun. It's another to take responsibility for the carnage they can create. But now? I find myself wishing for the familiar weight of my weapon strapped to my side.

Gun stores are a dime a dozen in Florida. I could purchase a new weapon, but if I used my badge to bypass the three-day waiting period, I'm positive an alert would be flagged at the Bureau. I'm not sure that I want that.

I think of the old revolver Butch used to keep in a metal lock box tucked away in his closet. I wonder if it's still there. I make a note to check when I get back to the house, but until then, I feel defenseless.

And backed into a corner.

Surprisingly enough, though my pulse races and a thick coat of sweat has sprung to the surface of my skin, the panic that has become so familiar lately doesn't take hold. I might have rage to thank for that. Because if I find out that someone had something to do with Butch's death—

I tell myself to calm down. There are a bunch of questions that need to be answered before I can determine that. Exiting the webpage, I access my call log, pressing the green button next to the first number I called this morning.

"Collier County Medical Examiner's Office. How may I direct your call?"

"Hi, yes. I need to speak with someone who can tell me my grandfather's cause of death."

"I'm afraid we can't give out that information over the phone."

"I'd be more than happy to come in and fill out whatever you need to release that information. Would that be something I could do today?"

"How long ago was your grandfather's death, honey?"

My voice cracks as I say, "Last Sunday."

"Hmm. There's a chance that the doctor's notes haven't been transcribed yet. What's his name?"

"Butch— I'm sorry. Charles Donovan."

The tapping of the receptionist's nails against her keyboard seems exceptionally loud as I wait.

"I'm sorry, sweetie, but we don't have any records on file for anyone by that name."

"What's that mean? That they haven't been transcribed yet, like you said?"

There's a long pause, filled only by the sound of my pulse in my ears.

"That means that his body was never brought to our office. He wasn't autopsied."

The words are like a physical blow, knocking the air from my lungs. If Butch wasn't autopsied that means that a physician signed off on his cause of death. Usually that happens when someone dies in a hospital, or under hospice care. But since he was found at home, that means he was sick and he knew it and didn't tell me. He didn't give me the chance to say goodbye.

"I see. Thank you," I say, my voice wavering as I end the call.

Had I really managed to mess everything up so badly that the one person who loved me in this world wanted nothing to do with me? Or am I missing something? Like how that corporate law firm comes into play.

I stare out the windshield, struggling to control my emotions, feeling like the crumpled husk of a dead palm frond that cartwheels by in the wind. A crow struts across the lawn fronting the funeral home. A shadow darkens the window as someone watches me from inside.

The need to know what happened to Butch is overwhelming. But it's going to have to wait.

My nerves are already on high alert. Having someone spy on me isn't helping. There's a grocery store parking lot down the road where I'll be more anonymous. Besides, since I'm already out of town, I might as well take advantage of the opportunity to grab some groceries now, so I don't have to do it later in Gator Glade.

The last thing I want is for everyone to know I'm back.

Putting the car in gear, I make the short drive to

the supermarket, parking under a tree at the far end of the lot. I glance around, double-checking that no one else is around before placing the call. Ringing fills my ear. Then a terse voice answers.

"Dr. Speck speaking."

"Yes, Dr. Speck, my name is Cassidy Knox. We spoke this morning about my grandfather, Charles Donovan."

"I remember. Were you not able to locate your grandfather's remains?" he asks.

"No, I was. But I had some additional questions that I was hoping you could help with."

"Such as?"

"Well, it appears that my grandfather wasn't autopsied."

"An autopsy isn't required in every situation."

"Yes, I'm aware. But I'm curious as to what his cause of death was determined to be."

"Hold on a minute."

Canned Muzak suddenly blares way too loud in my ear. I jerk the phone away, wincing. Debate putting the call on speaker, but a truck hauling a small white trailer has just pulled into a series of spaces alongside me. Paranoia makes me grit my teeth against the noise and deal with it until the doctor comes back on the line.

"The death certificate says myocardial infarction."

"A heart attack?"

"Yes."

"Was he seeing a cardiologist?"

There's a long pause before he says, "That's not information I have on hand."

"But you were the one to make the ruling, correct?"

"Ms. Knox, I understand that you're upset over

your loss, but I assure you, no mistakes were made."

"But how can you be sure?" When he doesn't reply, I say, "What did you base your findings on? I'd like a copy of the repor—"

I'm talking to myself. And according to the bars on the screen, it wasn't due to poor reception. I hit redial, but this time the call goes unanswered.

I throw the gearshift into reverse, planning on driving over to the hospital to demand answers face-to-face, but the time on the dash screen catches my eye. By the time I make it there, it will be after five. And it's Friday.

I hit the steering wheel with an irritated growl. Notice a man loitering by the truck that parked nearby, watching me as he smokes a cigarette.

There's no identifying information on either the vehicle or the trailer. Chances are he's a handyman, or maybe a landscaper, and yet, that little worried whisper in the back of my mind that's been kicked into overdrive wants to know—what if he's not?

What kind of reach might a law firm like Myers and Kleinman have? What lengths might they go to in order to keep a secret?

A shiver runs through me as I back out of my space and find a new one, this time much closer to the store, right in the center of constant activity. I watch in my rearview as the man gets back in his truck and drives off.

Exiting my car, I type up a quick email on the way inside. Send it to one of my colleagues, Mallory Chan. She's the only one at the Bureau that I'd consider a true friend. And I'm confident that she'll be able to find out what I need to know about that law office.

Something strange is going on here. Possibly something dangerous. Until I figure out what it is, I need to keep a low profile. I'm glad I decided to stop here instead of Gator Glade.

"Cassidy Knox?"

I freeze, squeezing the container of strawberries in my hand so hard that the top pops open.

"OMG, it is you, isn't it?"

Feeling like a deer in headlights, I look for the source of the voice. Feel a sinking sensation weigh down my limbs as I locate the speaker. Danielle Sims.

She was a couple grades behind me, but unless she's changed since we were in school, that whole low-profile plan I had? It's no longer an option. By the end of the day, everyone in Gator Glade will know that I'm back.

CHAPTER 8

Unlocking the door, I step into the house. Dump the grocery bags on the counter, then walk around, turning on the lights in all the rooms, checking to make sure I'm alone before returning to the kitchen and putting my items away. As I do, I can't help cataloguing the safety concerns of my location.

A house in the middle of nowhere. A property surrounded by swamp and woods. A windowpane within reaching distance of every lock. No wonder Butch never bothered with them.

If someone wanted in, they wouldn't have to try hard. The thought pushes a rush of adrenaline into my system.

I can't be here right now.

As useless as it seems, I lock the door behind me as I escape. Quicken my steps, every noise amplified as I hurry to the barn. Ducking inside, I sink to the ground, hugging my knees to my chest as I catch my breath.

I know that there's every chance that I'm being ridiculous. That I'm allowing the anxiety I already felt before I came down here to manifest into a mystery of wrongful death and unseen boogeymen. But what if I'm not?

I've learned the hard way not to ignore my gut. It's not a lesson I care to experience again.

A car door slams, and I flinch, knocking my head against the wall behind me. Scrambling to my feet, I scurry from stall to stall, peering through the back windows until I can see the source—a black truck parked just outside.

Jake.

With everything else that happened today, I'd forgotten about him, but his arrival instills me with renewed hope. He might have some of the answers I'm looking for. After all, he's been here helping Butch for the last two decades.

I comb my fingers through my hair. Brush the dirt off my shorts. Backhand the sheen of oil and sweat off my forehead just as a figure appears in the doorway, a dark smudge backlit by the sun.

"I thought I'd find you out here."

My breath catches. My pulse races. I take a step backward, then another. My foot snags on the water hose, making me stumble, my spine striking painfully against the wall as he steps inside.

A smirk stretches across Matt Kingston's face as he closes the distance between us.

"Long time no see, huh, Cass?" he asks.

Taking my chances with some faceless goon that may or may not exist suddenly has its appeal. I guess there's nothing like being cornered by your ex to put a bad situation into perspective. Especially when that ex is the reason you stayed away from your home for two decades, avoiding your past like a contagious disease.

"Weren't you going to let me know you were back in town?"

I dig deep, channeling the me I was, the one I hope to one day become again. The woman who wouldn't feel dizzy with panic right now. The me who wouldn't have to worry about finding her voice.

"I'm not back for a social call," I say.

He shrugs, making no efforts to hide the way his eyes roam up and down my body, checking me out. "I know. Just thought you might need a shoulder to cry on."

"I don't."

"Or another kind of comfort."

I wish I could claim to be shocked by his complete lack of empathy, tact, class, whatever you want to call that certain something that would keep a guy from propositioning a woman in mourning who he hasn't seen in twenty years. Unfortunately, I'd wasted most of my high school years with this loser. I know him well enough to expect otherwise.

To be honest, there's very little he could do that would surprise me, short of acting like a decent human being. I always thought it was a side effect of being a teenage boy whose father was the big sheriff of a tiny town. But it looks like being an entitled sleaze isn't something you grow out of.

"You thought wrong."

"Are you sure?"

"Yes. You should leave."

"Not yet." I wince as his palm hits the wall beside my head. "There's something we need to talk about first."

"I don't think there is."

I try to step to the side, but he puts his other hand on the wall, blocking my escape. He leans in, uncomfortably close, until I can feel the heat coming off his body.

"Well, I do."

I wonder what kind of charges I'd be looking at if I physically maimed him. Could I use what happened to me as part of my defense? I mean, technically I'm under psychiatric care. That has to count for something, right?

"Cass." I hold my breath as he brushes a strand of hair away from my face, readying myself to bolt, but unfortunately, he seems prepared for that, keeping me pinned in. "What happened between us? It wasn't fair. It wasn't what you think."

I know that it was exactly what I think. I took great pains to make sure that it was, though I don't say so.

"I didn't cheat on you."

He did. I just didn't care, not then, and not now.

"I just made it look like I did. For you. You see, I knew that you'd never leave for college, not with as good as things were between us. I just didn't realize that you'd be so hurt that you'd never come back. But nothing happened, babe. Honest. And now that you're here, I'm ready to forgive you for running away. There's no reason why we can't pick up right where we left off."

Except for the fact that he sickens me. I long to point out that you can't get into a good college on two weeks' notice. That my leaving had nothing to do with what happened, but I doubt he'd be able to wrap his narcissistic head around the truth.

"Matt, enough."

But he doesn't listen. He leans in closer, lowering his lips toward mine. I try to turn my head, but his arms have me locked in place. I get a hand between us, palm against his chest, trying to push him away.

Just as a voice says, "What's going on here?"

Matt drops his arms, jumping away from me. I cast a thankful look toward the doorway, where Tracey Vale, my best friend from school, stands beside Jake. Both wear tense expressions that confirm how bad what they walked in on looked.

"Tracey!" I hurry toward her, but the hate in her

expression stops me in my tracks.

"Well, Matt?" she asks.

"Nothing, babe. She just had something in her eye. She asked me to try and get it out."

My mouth drops open at the lie.

"Well, it's time to go. Now, Matt."

Spinning on her heel, she stomps outside, not giving me a single word. But based on what just happened, I don't need to guess which one she'd use.

"We'll finish this another time," Matt says in a low voice that only I can hear before following her.

I draw a shaky breath, my skin rippling as I watch him walk away. If I wasn't sure there was a real threat lurking in the shadows of Gator Glade before, I am now.

CHAPTER 9

The pizza Jake brought sits untouched on the desk in the tack room. His demeanor as he brushes past me as we go about giving the animals food and water is just as cold. And though I try to catch his eye every time the opportunity arises, he refuses to meet my gaze.

I feel guilty. I feel like I should apologize. But for what? I've done nothing wrong. He's the one stomping around like a toddler throwing a fit. The anger that accompanies the thought feels better than the guilt, so I go with it.

Jake opens a stall, balancing a stack of buckets. Stephano rushes past him, trotting up to me. Despite my mood, I can't help smiling. I squat to give him some scratches.

"If you think it's so cute, you can get him back in for the night. I don't have time for this."

Standing, I cross to the stall he's in, blocking the door with my body. "I have a question," I say.

"Or that," he mutters.

Pretending I didn't hear his comment, I continue, "What was going on with Butch?"

"What do you mean?"

"I mean medically."

He stops what he's doing and turns to face me. "You're his family. You tell me."

"I can't."

"Same here."

"So he never told you anything?" When he doesn't answer, I ask, "What about all the funeral arrangements he supposedly made?"

"What about them?"

"Are they legit? I looked up the law firm that's handling the estate, Myers and Kleinman. They're corporate attorneys. Why would they have anything to do with Butch's final arrangements?"

"Butch has been in this area his whole life. He had a lot of friends. Did you ever think that maybe one of them was doing him a favor?"

I shake my head, not buying it. "Butch did know a lot of people. He probably knew a half dozen lawyers who were better suited for something like drawing up an estate plan. I think there's something else going on here."

"Like what?"

"I'm not sure yet. But there's a lot that doesn't add up. I'm worried that Butch might have gotten himself in some kind of trouble."

"And you think his attorney had something to do with it? That what? They had him whacked?"

"For lack of a better term, yes. Maybe."

He squints at me like I'm microscopic. And that's how big I feel when he says, "Wow, if it's normal for an FBI agent to imagine conspiracies where there aren't any, no wonder the country's doing so well."

"You don't think it's odd that the whole funeral's been planned, everyone's been contacted, but his own granddaughter hasn't been notified yet?"

"Have you checked the mail?"

"What? Here?"

"Don't you think that would be a good place to start?"

"You think they'd send me something here?"

"It's common sense that you'd be staying here right now. I mean, I get why they'd think that you wouldn't bother to show, but—"

"What must you think of me, to say something like that?"

Tears sting my eyes, but I refuse to let them fall. I focus on the pain his words cause me. The shock. The shame.

Jake comes and stands in front of me, crossing his arms. Stephano dances in place between us, though neither of us gives him any attention.

"Where have you been the last twenty years, Cassidy? Not here. What am I supposed to think? Now if you don't mind, I've still got a ton of work to do. I've got to chase down Sam, the mule, and get him inside before it gets dark. Don't feel obligated to be here when I get back. I've got everything covered."

I step aside, my feelings reeling. "I thought you out of everyone would understand why I've stayed away."

"What's that supposed to mean?"

"Tell me, Jake. What is it you think you walked in on earlier?"

"Oh, it seemed pretty clear to me what was going on."

"Really? So it looked like I was enjoying myself?"

"It didn't look like you were putting up a fight."

"Yeah, because assaulting the sheriff's son, even in self-defense, would really go over well, wouldn't it?" My voice is rising, I can't stop it. "I thought if anyone knew what kind of power Sherrif Kingston holds in Gator Glade, it would be you. But I guess I was wrong. He must not have been harassing you back when we were in school. You must have deserved all those petty charges."

He frowns. "What are you trying to say?"

"I'm letting you know why I was afraid to come back home!" I yell. I draw a deep breath. Exhale slowly. My voice wavers as I say, "Butch knew. He knew what I had to go through to get away, and he knew what I'd have to deal with if I ever came back. Sheriff Kingston made it perfectly clear to me when I was sixteen."

"You didn't leave until you were eighteen."

"Exactly. I spent two years planning my escape. Making sure that when I did leave, the repercussions wouldn't fall on Butch. But you just go ahead and judge me. It seems to be something you excel at."

I hear him calling my name as I storm off, but I quicken my steps instead of stopping. I need to get away, fast, before he has a chance to see the tears streaming down my face. The self-doubt in my expression. Because a small part of me is scared he might be right.

Not about staying away the last twenty years, that was Butch's decision as much as mine, but about Myers and Kleinman. About a medical issue that Butch knew about but didn't share. About imagining monsters where there aren't any, so I don't have to face my own.

I keep marching past the house, down the driveway, all the way until I reach the road. The ancient mailbox groans as I jerk it open. I pull out the stack of mail inside, but even before I flip through it, embarrassment heats my cheeks.

The manilla envelope is thick. And it bears the emblem of the law offices of Myers and Kleinman.

It's getting dark. I tell myself I should go inside, but my feet remain rooted to the spot. I can't move. Not as the mosquitoes feast on me. Not as my stomach growls. Not as a truck races past on the road beside me, entirely too close for comfort.

The throaty chorus of bullfrogs mocks me as I stand there, frozen with the realization that I was wrong. All those threads I'd seen, the connections I'd made, they weren't real. Which makes me worry—what else might I have imagined?

CHAPTER 10

It feels like I'm walking through quicksand as I rush through the house, tracking down my purse, carrying my coffee mug to the kitchen, rinsing it and putting it in the sink. Studiously keeping my gaze averted from the envelope that sits on the table. The one from the law offices of Myers and Kleinman. The one I've yet to open.

I promise myself that when I get home from the funeral, I'll sit and see what's inside. Then I'll start calling around for new homes for the animals. There's a whole network of rescues that Butch was friendly with. I'm sure at least a few of them would be willing to help.

Worst case scenario, I'll make some of the calls from the road after I leave. It's not like Jake's opinion of me could get any lower. Not that it matters. I have a life and a home and a career to get back to.

The tension in my temples clamps down like a vice, making my head throb. Who am I kidding?

Lying to myself is a skill I never properly developed. The truth is that I have a cramped, overpriced apartment and a job that may already no longer exist.

It's not much of a life, and it hasn't been for quite some time. But at least there, I'm anonymous. No one gets to judge me for the stupid mistakes I made as a teen.

Putting on my sunglasses, I step out into the sweltering heat, lock the door, and jog to my car, already eager to be back in the air conditioning. I spin the dial to full blast and turn the thermostat to the lowest setting, not wanting to soak my dress with sweat.

I already look like enough of a wreck, my face red and puffy from a night spent crying instead of sleeping. The last thing I need is to set tongues wagging with my appearance.

Nerves churn inside my stomach at the thought of who I might see today. Though Butch was generally beloved by everyone who knew him, I have more foes than friends in the area. And that was before I took off and didn't show my face for two decades.

I wish that I wasn't heading into this alone. That I had an ally I could count on to have my back. Instead, I have a headache and a bad case of the jitters from drinking an entire pot of coffee by myself this morning.

My eyes feel dry and gritty as I stare at the road in front of me, hands tightening on the wheel as the rural single lane road spreads into three lanes in each direction. I didn't notice yesterday how bad traffic had grown as you near Naples, but I'd been working on a half night's sleep then. Now, the deficit has grown to the point where my entire body feels the effects.

It makes me feel old.

It seems like just yesterday that I was planning my escape. To be honest, I thought I'd have accomplished more with my life by now. It's like I've been running in place all these years, always part of the race but at the same time, always bringing up the rear.

And I'm tired. I'm almost forty. Life should be easier by now.

Pulling into the parking lot at the funeral home, I give myself a last-minute pep talk. It's okay that I don't have kids. That I'm single. That most of my time with the FBI has been spent behind a desk, poring over data in a windowless room.

There are worse things. Besides, no one knows the truth. I could walk inside and spin a new narrative, one that makes my life seem like something worth envying. It's just too bad I don't have enough energy to make up anything good.

Though I had purposely forced myself to time my arrival so I wouldn't be too early, the doors to the funeral home are closed. A crowd has gathered out front. Small groups squeeze into the few patches of shade. I scan their faces through my windows.

Many are familiar, like Donna, who runs the feed store, or Franklin, the mechanic who kept Butch's ancient farm equipment running. I doubt they'd remember me. These are the people I need to hide behind, because others, like Mrs. Healy, my eighth-grade teacher, need to be avoided at all costs.

And Jake.

I duck my head though he appears too preoccupied with the conversation he's part of to notice my arrival. But I'm not the only one to notice him. It seems like every woman under fifty is casting glances in his direction. It's easy to see why.

Though I doubt anyone would complain about the way he looks in jeans and a T-shirt, he cuts an impressive figure in the suit he's wearing. Probably because it's an impressive suit. Even from a distance it looks expensive. Tailored. And it makes me feel incredibly suspicious.

Exactly what does he do to afford something like that? Maybe I got it wrong last night about Sheriff Kingston picking on him. Maybe the sheriff was right.

I'm still wondering when the door finally opens, the same gaunt, expressionless man I spoke with yesterday appearing briefly to say a few words before retreating. Inhaling deeply, I brace myself, then exit my vehicle and step straight into the fray, keeping my head down as I join the exodus streaming inside.

Almost immediately, I hear my name. My skin bristles as I look for the source, knowing that I should have expected this. That it was too much to hope to keep a low profile. But as my gaze lands on a familiar face, this one friendly, I realize that I just got my first break of the day.

"Gordon Massey?"

"Yeah."

"Wow, I almost didn't recognize you. You look great!"

"So do you." He gives me a bashful smile. It vanishes an instant later as he says, "I just wish I was seeing you under different circumstances."

I have no idea how to respond, so I don't.

"How long are you back in town for?" he asks, falling into step beside me.

"I'm not sure yet. Probably not long."

"Well, you'll have to let me buy you that drink I owe you before you leave."

It takes me a moment to figure out what he's talking about. Gordon was my science partner all four years of high school. The three years of required courses, and then, because he was such a good guy and one of my closest friends, he did me the favor of enrolling in the extra class I elected to take senior year.

A nightmarish extra class with a grueling workload. He'd been sure we were going to fail. I'd assured him we wouldn't. He promised to buy me a drink at the local bar as soon as we were old enough if I was right. We'd passed, but I was gone long before we were of legal drinking age.

"It's a deal," I say, wondering if I mean it.

I should. He's one of the few people I have fond memories of from Gator Glade. Even now, he's trying to look out for me. I pretend not to notice as he shoots looks of disapproval toward the audience we've drawn, some of whom are blatantly staring.

But it's too late.

A ripple of conversation travels through the mourners ahead of us. The guests part, stepping to the side, clearing the way to the front of the line. Swallowing hard, I nod my appreciation, moving forward though I'm not yet ready to approach the casket at the head of the room.

All too soon I'm there.

I'm surprised to find that Butch had opted for an open casket. Even more so at the wave of absolute grief that crashes against me as I peer down at him. He looks so peaceful, almost like he's sleeping, but so much older than he'd appeared the last time I saw him. Has it really been that long?

I recognize the suit he's chosen as the same one he wore to my college graduation. The button-down shirt is a pale blue that would have perfectly matched his eyes if they were open. But something's wrong.

His shirt collar is buttoned all the way to the top. He would have hated that.

Though I know he's beyond caring, it feels like something that will haunt me for years to come if I don't correct it. So I reach down and undo the top button, rearranging his shirt collar.

And freeze.

I blink hard, sure that my fatigued eyes must be seeing wrong, but when they open again, it's still there. A one-inch-thick raspberry-colored mark wraps around the base of his throat, perfectly uniform other than a rectangular anomaly slightly off to the side.

I lean in for a closer look. Shift his shirt, trying to get a look at the whole thing. I can't. The bruise appears to encircle his entire neck. And no matter how hard I try, I can think of only one thing that could have caused it—a ligature of some kind.

Which means Butch's cause of death? It wasn't a heart attack.

CHAPTER 11

I'm sure everyone thought that the startled expression on my face as I hurried to the back of the room was a direct result of seeing Butch in his casket—at least, that's what I keep telling myself. Because I feel like I dropped the ball. Like I should have studied the faces of those I passed to see what they revealed. To see if maybe someone looked like they might have known the real reason for my shock.

Some FBI agent I am.

To be fair, it's not like I'm a field agent. I always wanted to be. That was my intention when I joined the Bureau. But fate had other plans for me.

You see, there are computer programs used to troll the hundreds of thousands of cases reported by various law enforcement agencies across the country, looking for relationships between them. And while I'm sure that there are many actual connections that the algorithm probably misses, there are also many that get flagged that really shouldn't be.

The decision of which ones get pursued falls to a task force of agents who pore over this information to see if there appears to be a real link that warrants investigating. For over a decade, that's what I did. It's what I excelled at. I was so successful at identifying legitimate leads, even when the initial connection between cases seemed weak, that I pigeonholed myself straight out of training.

It wasn't a hard task to be good at. It just took a bit of effort. Spending two days on a hit spit out by the algorithm instead of an hour. Taking the time to delve into the details of the cases. Contacting the investigating officers to ask a few questions. All things that could be done from my desk.

But I always wanted more.

Turns out I should have been happy with what I had, a job I excelled at, a department I came to lead despite my age and lack of experience conducting an actual investigation. Instead, I did everything I could to land a position that would lead to my escape from that stuffy room with no windows.

And once I finally succeeded, look what happened—I didn't even make it a year before disaster struck, taking my partner's life and almost costing my own.

None of that comes into play now, though, as I pace the undertaker's office. No one knows that I have a connection to any form of police work. Butch thought it best to keep it that way, and I can't say that I disagree.

Small towns can be funny about things like that, especially when their main contact with law enforcement is a corrupt, bigoted old fool like Sheriff Kingston. Yet, for some reason, Butch shared the truth with Jake. I push the question why out of my mind and turn toward the gaunt man slumped behind the desk.

"And you noticed the mark?"

"Again, yes."

"But you didn't think of mentioning it to anyone?"

"As I told you before, I wasn't privy to your grandfather's cause of death. It's not my job to question things. When remains come my way, my job is to help their family lay them to rest."

I check my watch, then resume pacing. It's been over an hour since I informed the undertaker that the burial part of the funeral would be canceled, pending an investigation. And since I called the medical examiner's office, demanding that they send one of their medicolegal investigators over to collect the body.

The undertaker hadn't been happy about it, had flat out told me that my grief was understandable, but my suspicions were unfounded. So I've been expending my energy by stalking back and forth across this tiny room instead of inflicting violence. Because that bruising around Butch's neck? That's not the result of a heart attack.

Someone's gone to a lot of trouble to keep the truth concealed. As far as I'm concerned, everybody's a suspect.

A tap sounds on the door behind me. I spin to face it as it opens. A man somewhere in his fifties with darkly tanned, weathered skin sticks his head inside, checking the room before entering.

"Oscar," he says, nodding to the man behind the desk.

"Rich," the undertaker greets back.

"Why don't you tell me what's going on here?"

Irritation boils beneath my skin at being ignored. It grows with the undertaker's weary sigh. "This is the decedent's granddaughter. She saw some mark on the body she thought was suspicious and insisted on making the call."

The man named Rich turns an annoyed grimace thinly veiled by sympathy my way. "Ma'am—"

The decision is made in an instant, before I really think about it. It's out there too fast to take it back.

"Agent."

Reaching into my purse, I remove my wallet and flip it open to my Bureau identification. "Special Agent Cassidy Knox."

Oscar clears his throat, straightening in his seat at the look the detective shoots him.

"Rich Bailey," he says, finally taking the time to introduce himself.

I ignore him, saying, "There is what appears to be a ligature mark around my grandfather's neck."

"I checked before I left to come here. Our office didn't autopsy the body."

"That's correct, although I have no idea why not."

"Ma'am. Agent. If the physician treating your grandfather was willing to sign off on his death certificate, then that means he was confident about what happened. Perhaps the mark you saw was a result of resuscitative efforts."

I smile, though there's nothing nice about it.

"I was told my grandfather was discovered deceased by a friend who visited the house. As far as I'm aware, no resuscitative efforts were administered, but I fail to see how they would have resulted in a bruise encircling his entire neck. And before you suggest that it stemmed from whatever affliction the attending physician was treating him for, I was informed his cause of death was ruled a heart attack, though to my knowledge he was not receiving treatment from a cardiologist."

I don't mention that I have no idea what doctors Butch *was* receiving care from, if any. As far as I'm concerned, it doesn't matter.

The investigator glances at the undertaker, who doesn't refute my story. "I assume that the body has been cleaned and embalmed?"

"Yes."

He turns his attention back to me. "Any trace that was on the body will be gone. Do you know who would have jurisdiction?"

"Sheriff Kingston."

His grimace matches my own. "I can tell you right now, he won't touch it. Not without any evidence to lay the groundwork for an investigation."

"I've already called the state police requesting a detective. I'd prefer to keep the sheriff out of this, if possible."

"A detective won't be assigned until we confirm there's a case."

"If signs consistent with strangulation are found, that's enough evidence to open a case, correct?"

"Correct."

"Then perform the autopsy," I say. "As next of kin, I have the right to request one. This is me making that request. We'll worry about the rest when we get to it."

The thought of staying in Gator Glade longer than I have to strikes a match inside me, lighting the burner beneath that pot of panic that's been on a constant simmer within my chest. My muscles draw tight, making my breaths shallow. But the attack fails to take hold.

Everything I had has been taken from me by monsters. My courage. My confidence. My sense of well-being. My ability to do something as simple as close my eyes without feeling fear.

And now my grandfather.

I'm tired of feeling powerless. It's got to stop.

And it will. I'm going to find out who killed Butch. And then I'm going to make them pay.

CHAPTER 12

I'm afraid I'm not a very good hostess. As soon as I had what I needed—a promise that Butch's body would be transferred to the medical examiner's office as soon as the viewing was over—I took off. It might not be the most considerate thing I've ever done, leaving the undertaker to explain why the burial part of the funeral was canceled without revealing the truth, but I tell myself it's part of his job.

It's like a kindergarten teacher having to deal with glue. A sports coach having to smell sweat. Or an FBI agent coming in contact with a killer. It comes with the territory.

Only this time, the game's on my home turf. And I'm the one who's hunting.

Which is why I had to leave. The raw aggression I feel brewing in the pit of my stomach as I prepare for battle isn't exactly helpful for dealing with an endless procession of sympathy and well-wishers, especially when one of them might be the one I'm looking for.

There's too much noise in my head for that, the static almost deafening as I try to make sense of what's happening, still not quite believing what I saw. What it means.

But it's the why that's really doing a number on me. Because Butch was a wonderful person. He never hurt anyone in his life. Who could have possibly wanted him dead?

I pull into the driveway, grateful to have finally made it back, but the relief that I feel is short-lived as the barn comes into view. I glance at the house, thinking about Butch's gun, wishing I knew exactly where it was, or even better, that I had it on me now as I hit the gas, a cloud of dust rising up as I veer onto the grass to loop around the truck hitched to an empty horse trailer parked in my path.

Turning the wheel, I spin sideways, blocking the entrance to the barn, making the man who was heading inside jump back. The words he says in response are easy to read on his lips, but when I open the door and get out of my car, he's all pleasantry and smiles.

"Hi there," he says. "I'm Jeff Gates. It's a pleasure to meet you, Ms.—?"

I stare down at his proffered hand but don't take it. Or offer my name. Instead, I say, "Did you notice the NO TRESSPASSING sign out front, Mr. Gates? You had to drive right past it to get here."

His smile flickers, replaced for a moment with annoyance before he manages to pull it back in place.

"I'd have called first, but I didn't know what number to try, what with Butch being gone and all."

"You knew Butch?"

"I surely did."

"Were you aware that he was being buried today?"

The coldness in his eyes lets me know that he was, even though he ignores the question. "I came to talk about taking that zebra off your hands."

Sometimes it's best to fight fire with fire. Wanting to prove that I can play dumb too, I ask, "What zebra?"

This time when his smile falters, he doesn't manage to retrieve it.

"The one you've got in that barn over there, little lady."

"That barn right there?" I point behind me. "The one on private property?"

"Listen, now. I was hoping it wouldn't come to this, but with Butch gone, so is the exotic animal permit holder. We can get the authorities involved if you want, but they're just going to end up giving me the animal, so you might as well save yourself the headache and hassle and hand her over now."

"Who'd you say you are again?"

"Jeff Gates, owner of Surfing Safari Animal Experience. I assure you we'll take good care of her. I'll even give you a couple of free passes so you can come visit, if you'd like?"

"Well, Jeff, I'm Special Agent Cassidy Knox with the FBI, and I assure you, that won't be necessary, because you won't be taking any animals off this property."

"I'm afraid this matter is out of your jurisdiction. This is a matter for the Florida Fish and Wildlife Commission."

"And I'm afraid you're just wasting your time and mine. Go ahead and call the FWC. Please. I can guarantee that they don't think any better of you than Butch did. He'd come back from the dead before he'd let you take a cockroach off this property to that slaughterhouse you run."

"Be that as it may—"

"Stop. Talking."

I take a step toward him in such a manner that he takes a step back, which is the smartest thing he's done since I've met him, because I really feel like I could hurt someone right now.

"My grandfather hated people like you. That's why he dedicated his life to this sanctuary—to keep animals out of hands like yours. It's also why I've had a Class III exotics permit since I was sixteen."

For the first time, the pompous puff to his chest deflates. "Grandfather?"

"That's right. Now get back in your vehicle and don't come back. I'll be calling the sheriff to file a complaint as soon as I've sent him a photo of you and your license plate from my surveillance footage. If I ever catch you on this property again, I'll be pressing charges."

I follow him as he retreats to his truck, not willing to cede a single inch to this man. Stand there with my arms crossed, glaring at him as he opens his door. He turns and gives me a surly look.

It's all the inspiration I need to add, "Oh, and Mr. Gates? You can get any thoughts you have about that zebra out of your head. You're never going to get her. In fact, I'm going to text my lawyer right now and have her draft an amendment to my will naming at least a half dozen people who would inherit her if I were no longer able to provide her care. Just in case."

I hold up my phone for emphasis, keep it raised as he drives entirely too fast toward the road. And though I don't have a lawyer, or a will, or even surveillance equipment to film the footage I just lied about, I text the name of every person I can think of capable of taking Daisy to Mallory Chan back in Virginia. Again, just in case.

Because everyone loved Butch—except for a handful of scum who'd had animals removed from their custody and placed into my grandfather's care. And I'm pretty sure that Jeff Gates was one of them.

It might not seem like much of a motive, but people have been killed for less. And my opinion of anyone who mistreats an animal is lower than low. Which means that as of right now, that man is a suspect. And keeping Daisy safe is one of my main priorities.

CHAPTER 13

Though the sun has been down for hours, the air is still thick and humid. I feel sticky as I sit on the hardpacked dirt floor of the barn, listening to the sound of the frogs sing in the nearby swamp, the crickets humming along. But it's not just the insects and the amphibians and my own tortured thoughts keeping me company—Stephano is curled against my thigh, napping.

I raise the bottle in my hand, taking a long fiery swig. When I lower it again, I've been joined by more company. This time human.

Jake stands several yards away, staring at me. I assume he's debating if it would be rude to run away since he's been spotted. I gesture for him to go, giving him an out.

"Everything's under control here. Everyone's been fed and watered. You get the night off."

Instead of leaving, he steps closer.

"You okay?"

"I'm fine."

Surprisingly, I am. As odd as it seems, having a purpose as important as finding my grandfather's killer has done wonders for my inner strength. Well that, and enough alcohol to burn away any weakness that remained, as well as most of my stomach lining.

"Tough day," he remarks

"Yep."

And he doesn't even know the half of it.

"Want to talk about it?"

"Nope."

He moves closer, enough so that his shadow falls over me. I keep my attention firmly focused on the wall ahead, refusing to look at him.

"Listen, I'm sorry about last night. Really sorry. I had a bad day and I took it out on you. Said some things that I shouldn't have."

"Or maybe you should have."

He sighs, knees cracking as he squats beside me. "You don't mean that."

"Maybe I do. We both know I deserved it. Or maybe it's just the first bottle talking."

I slide my eyes over to his, which are looking at the glass container clutched in my hand.

"First?"

"Don't worry. It wasn't full. And I have a high tolerance."

He lowers himself the rest of the way to the ground, taking a seat beside me. "Yeah, I remember that about you."

"What's that supposed to mean?" I ask, frowning. I'm not one of those stereotypes, the alcoholic law enforcement official. I don't drink on a regular basis. There are times I go months between drinks. But when I do imbibe, I have a habit of binging. Not the thing I'm most proud of, but I have too many faults for it to be the least.

"Don't tell me you don't remember drinking everyone under the table back in school."

"I do. I just don't see how you know."

"Because you used to drive me crazy trying to keep an eye on you, making sure you stayed safe."

"Oh please. You didn't know I existed."

He stares at me until I have no choice but to meet his eyes. I swallow hard at what I see.

"I assure you that I did, and not just because we used to play together when we were little. It's a small town. Kind of hard not to notice the smartest and prettiest girl in it."

"Now I know you're full of it. What about Lauren Groff? Or Taylor Ott?"

"They were intelligent and attractive but not like you. You were in a category of your own. Still are."

I snort my disbelief.

"Cassie." It's what he used to call me when we were little. The familiarity of it thaws me a bit. Enough to get me to look at his outstretched hand.

Reluctantly, I pass him the bottle, deciding that if he tries to keep it from me, I'll attack, which is definitely the booze thinking. Instead, he takes a long slug. Then, in a low voice he asks, "Did Sheriff Kingston really threaten you?"

"Only if you count being told about all the bad things that would happen if a piece of swamp trash like me ever tried to break up with his precious little prince a threat."

He curses and takes another drink. "I'm sorry about that."

"Yeah, me too." I trace the outline of a muddy hoofprint Stephano left on my leg with a fingertip. "Did you really keep an eye on me in high school?"

"Yes."

"Did you really think I was pretty?"

"Absolutely."

"Then why didn't you ever talk to me?"

"Because I was seventeen and you were fourteen. It made me feel like a dirty pervert. And by the time you got a little older…"

I was dating Matt. It's one more reason to hate my younger self.

I hold my hand out for the bottle, feeling relief that I won't have to choose violence when he gives it to me. After a couple of swallows, I say, "I had the biggest crush on you back then."

The silence between us is absolute. I wish I had kept my mouth shut. My cheeks burn with embarrassment. I raise the bottle to my lips, but his hand on my arm stops me before I can take a sip.

"Just back then?" he asks. "Does that mean you don't anymore?"

I'm speechless. And he… he's leaned closer to me. Lowered his head toward mine. Is looking at me with eyes filled with such intensity that my cheeks feel like they might catch fire, only this time it's not because I feel awkward.

My pulse races as I turn to face him. He's so close that I can smell the faint trace of soap on his skin. Can see the pale, jagged scar on his jawline from where he got snagged by a piece of barbed wire while trying to duck through the neighbor's fence to retrieve a ball when he was seven. I raise my hand to run my fingers over it when a noise shatters the moment, bringing us both to our feet.

"What was that?" he asks.

I'm already running down the aisle behind Stephano as the awakened goat heads toward Daisy's stall.

"It's time," I call over my shoulder, even though I can hear his steps thudding behind me. "The baby's coming."

He draws to a halt beside me at the stall door.

"It sounded like it was already here."

Daisy rolls her eyes in our direction from her spot on the ground. Her side stretches like there's an alien inside trying to elbow its way out. The noise comes again—loud and shrill, bone chillingly eerie.

"Sometimes they start whinnying before they've managed to be born."

I open the door, intending to go inside, but she flashes her teeth at me.

"It's okay, girl," I say in a soft voice, closing it again but leaving the bolt undone in case I need to get in there quickly. "You're okay. I'll stay out here."

"I texted the vet," Jake says from beside me.

"I don't think he's going to make it in time."

"Will that be a problem?"

"Not if everything goes well."

"Then let's hope it does. He just responded."

"And?"

"He's out of town tonight. Said he could stop by sometime tomorrow to check on the foal."

"Just great," I mutter, running through the handful of births I've helped with over the years—none of which have been in the last two decades. I silently cheer Daisy on, hoping she'll be able to manage on her own.

But the tiny hoof that emerges a moment later lets me know that she won't.

"Is that?" Jake asks.

"Yes."

The angle and thickness of the cannon, the lower part of the leg, lets us know that we're looking at a hind limb. The baby needs to be turned, quickly, or both Daisy and her foal will be in trouble.

I swallow hard, heart beating so loudly I can barely hear myself think. But my voice is deceptively calm as I ask, "Do you know if Butch has any sleeves out here?”

"I’ll go get them.”

I draw deep breaths as I wait for Jake to return with a box of shoulder-length gloves. When he does, I can’t meet his gaze as I pull a pair on, afraid that he’ll see my fear. My doubt. Because, although I know what needs to be done, I’m not sure that I can do it. And if I can’t, I’m not just failing myself.

This time, when I open the stall door, all Daisy does is roll her eyes. The whites flash. Foam gathers around her mouth. Sweat froths along her neck.

Careful of her hooves, I lower myself to the ground behind her. Move her tail out of the way. Take the tiny hoof in my hand and gently fold it back inside her, following with my arms.

I feel around blindly. Find the foal’s head and guide it around, using my other hand to push against its rump. Once I have the baby in the correct position, I locate its front hooves and pull them out as I withdraw my arms. Then I quickly stand, pulling the gloves off as I retreat from the stall.

Daisy grunts. Jake’s hand curls around my arm. I hear him swallow loudly. We both wince, glancing away from the miracle of birth.

Then it’s over. Though Daisy deserves most of the credit, I’m filled with pride and disbelief at the small part I played. I can’t believe I did it.

The new mother rocks to her hooves, nuzzling her foal, a filly. I hold my breath while we wait for the little girl to get her gangly legs under her to try and stand.

The baby before me does not look like a half-breed. She looks like a pure zebra. Which would make her worth a lot of money for someone wanting to capitalize off her. Up to forty years’ worth of profits.

Definitely enough to kill for.

The filly makes it up, and the dark thoughts momentarily flee my head as she finds her way and begins to nurse. I turn to Jake, grinning. Find him already looking at me.

I feel like I should say something, but then we're doing something better than talking. I couldn't tell you who made the move, or if we both did. I'm not sure I could even tell you my name.

Because that little alarm bell that's been going off inside my head since I woke up in that basement has finally fallen silent. I want to enjoy every second of peace brought about by the surprising softness of his lips. The press of his body against mind. The heat of his palms through my shirt as his arms wrap around me, pulling me closer.

But as his right hand travels up my back, the siren starts again. Softly at first. I try to block it out, hoping it will stop. Instead, it grows louder as his fingertips brush against the raw edges of my wound.

It's been too long since I've done this. I can't breathe, and the claxon is going off too loud now for me to think clearly enough to figure it out. Pressing my hand against his chest, I hold him in place as I pull my mouth away, gasping for air.

"I'm sorry. I should go."

"No, Jake—"

But it's already too late.

I watch helplessly as he hurries from the barn. Swallow against the lump in my throat as his truck's engine thunders to life. Wonder why I always make the wrong decision as the sound fades until it's swallowed by the night.

Once again, I'm alone, not just in the barn but in this life and in the fight I've signed up for. Because I've got a killer to find and a couple of zebras to protect, and if I was going to share about either battle I was facing, it would have been with Jake, right?

Yet I hadn't said a word. I suppose that's my answer. The same one as who to trust.

CHAPTER 14

It's going to be a scorcher. Though the day is still young, the air feels like stew, hot and thick, chunky if you count the flying insects that stick to the sweat coating my skin. My insides are just as much of a sloppy mess as my outsides, yet as I lean against the fence, chin propped on my forearms as I watch Daisy and her baby in the pasture, the only thing that matters is how I'm going to keep them safe.

Not just them, but all the animals here that my grandfather dedicated his life to protecting. From Stephano, the goat, and Chomp, the gator, to the cow and the pigs and the mule and even—I glance at the pelican eyeing me from his perch on the fence post beside me— the fowl.

I know what Butch would want. Now I just have to figure out what I want.

I'm so sidetracked by my internal debate that I don't notice the black truck coming down the drive until it's too late for me to escape. Is it Jake? Matt? Someone else? Not knowing which would be worse, my body tenses as I turn to face it, waiting for the driver to make an appearance.

The door opens. Relief crashes over me as Jake emerges. It's followed a second later by the sting of the hurt I was forced to swallow down last night, the injury still tender.

I push away from the fence, intending to get back to work, but there's nothing left to do. That's the only positive side effect of insomnia coupled with boundless nervous energy—you can accomplish a lot in the time before you crash.

I've made it back to the barn, yet I'm not quite inside when he catches up with me. I grab the hose so I have something in my hand, a task I can pretend to do, and spray the mud pit I'd made for the pigs to wallow in this morning, though it's still plenty wet.

"Hey."

I ignore Jake as he comes to stand beside me.

"I'm sorry about last night. Again."

"It's fine."

"Is it? You won't look at me."

I lift my eyes to his just to be contrary and prove him wrong. "What do you expect?"

"You're right. I—"

But now that I've started, I don't want to stop. Interrupting him, I say, "I wasn't trying to push you away last night. I just, it's been a long time. I forgot how to…"

And now I regret saying anything at all. I press my lips together, hard. Pinch the inside of my cheek between my molars and grind down.

"Forgot how to what? You seemed to know what you were doing. Very well, in fact."

"I forgot how to time my breathing," I admit, though I don't share what triggered me to become breathless in the first place.

Jake laughs. "Well, if it makes you feel any better, I didn't notice. And that's not why I left."

"Then why did you?"

Dropping the hose, I turn to face him fully, not wanting to sound whiny, or to be needy, but I need to know. The abrupt way he left last night, it felt like a rejection. It hurt, even if I don't want to admit it.

"Because Butch trusted me. He made me promise to look after you."

"And?"

"And I'm not sure that what happened last night was what he had in mind."

"Let me tell you something about Butch. He didn't raise me to be the type of woman who needs someone to take care of her." I ignore the tiny voice telling me to take a closer look at my reality lately. Because it's my voice, which means I can tell myself to shut up without worrying about being rude.

Jake smiles patiently, like I'm a kid who just said something cute. It makes me feel like growling. I swear, I've never met someone who drove me so crazy before. Who makes me yoyo so fast between like and loathing that I feel like I'm suffering from whiplash. Had he always been like this?

Thinking about it, I swear I remember having this feeling as a child. It's possible I'm imagining it, but as he tentatively touches my arm, instantly erasing my desire to push him in the mud and replacing it with the urge to kiss him, I lean toward believing it's true.

"Butch wouldn't have asked me if I didn't know that."

"Then what do you think he meant?"

Jake shrugs, but he seems to have an answer pretty fast. "You know. Watch out for you. Have your back if you get into any trouble."

It makes me wonder exactly what that grandfather of mine knew—about my fate and his own. Had he suspected someone was going to kill him?

Stephano comes running over from whatever adventure he's been having. Scooping him up, I use the tiny goat to hide my face as I say, "Well, you're off the hook. I'm fine. No trouble to need rescuing from."

It's a lie, but it's not. I know I'm a mess. But this isn't something anyone else can fix for me.

I need to be the one to find the truth about what really happened to Butch. Just like I'm the only one who can patch the holes made by the pieces of myself that I left in that basement. And I shouldn't be letting myself get distracted from either of those goals.

Jake takes the goat from my arms and gently sets him on the ground. "Then maybe I should make some."

"Has anyone ever told you that you're infuriating?"

"Yes. This feisty little girl who used to boss me around when I was younger. Apparently, I didn't get enough of it back then, because I'm back for more now."

I stare at him, telling myself not to cut him a break no matter how badly I want to. Call it a matter of pride. *Or maybe woman's intuition*, my inner voice whispers.

"Cassie, I'm sorry. I know I keep doing things that cause me to say that and I'm sorry about that, too."

"I'm not sure why we're having this conversation. You don't owe me any apologies."

"Maybe I'm hoping you'll take pity on me and give me another shot?"

"At what?" I ask.

"Another kiss?" he suggests, stepping forward and closing the space between us. His palm is warm against my cheek. His stroke soft despite the roughness of his calluses as it drifts down to cup my neck. I tip my face up to meet his.

Whoop, whoop.

We spring apart like a couple of teenagers caught by a parent as the first of two police cruisers blips its siren, emerging from a cloud of dust as it races down the drive. Both of us curse as Sheriff Kingston pries his bulk from behind the wheel. His hand rests on the gun holstered to his side as he comes toward us, the officer who'd been in the second vehicle following close on his heels.

"I heard I'd find you here."

"There something I can help you with, Sheriff?" I ask.

He ignores me, addressing Jake as he says, "I have some questions for you, son." Gesturing toward the other officer, he says, "Jed here's gonna give you a ride down to the station to answer them."

Jake's body goes rigid, his shoulders rising up under his ears. He might be an adult now, but some things you don't outgrow—like your response to the person who abused their authority to repeatedly harass you when you were a kid. I know, because my own memories of being mistreated by this man are still raw wounds I carry with me.

"On what grounds?" Jake asks.

"On the grounds that we need to talk about some trouble that went down last night."

"Jake was here," I say, crossing my arms as I step forward. "With me."

Sheriff Kingston's nose wrinkles, his eyes narrowing as he looks me up and down, his expression betraying what he thinks about me, what he's always thought. I know because he once flat out told me, and though that was many years ago, his words still ring in my ears. They still sting.

Well, good. Hopefully that means he'll keep his son away from me.

"All night?" he asks, the implication clear in his tone.

"Butch's zebra went into labor. The vet couldn't make it. Jake helped me with the birth."

If the sheriff noticed that I didn't answer his question, he doesn't let on. Instead, he asks, "You sure about that?"

I gesture toward the paddock, at the obviously newly born filly balancing on splayed legs as she nurses.

The sheriff grunts. "What about your truck? You let anyone borrow it?"

"Not that I know of," Jake says. "What's this all about?"

"Grace Billie."

"Grace? Is she okay?"

"Well, no, son, she's not. Seems someone decided to choke the life out of her during the early hours this morning, though I suspect you already know that." Jake inhales so sharply that I almost don't hear the sheriff's next words. "I have two different neighbors who swear that they saw your truck parked outside while it happened."

It takes every ounce of willpower I have not to turn to look at Jake, to study his reaction. I freeze the expression on my face, trying hard to remember what time he left here last night, but I never checked the time. I stayed busy until after dawn broke, trying to distract myself from the abrupt way he left.

Had he gone straight home afterward? Or had he made a stop, possibly to vent his frustration?

My thoughts drift to the seconds before the sheriff arrived, when Jake's hand had lowered from my cheek to my neck. Had there been anything ominous about it? At the time, no, but in retrospect, had his thumb been too close to the tender hollow at the base of my throat? My skin burns where the warmth of Jake's palm had been just a short time ago.

"They said they recognized your vehicle from when you dated the victim. You did date the victim, didn't you?"

Jake sounds winded as he says, "Yeah." His voice a little stronger as he adds, "A few years ago. She's been married and divorced since."

"We already checked the ex out. His truck's red. They said the truck was black, like yours. You drive a different vehicle back then?"

"No."

"Did these neighbors get a plate number?" I ask.

"If they had, we wouldn't be standing here talking. I'd have hauled him in already."

The way he says it, it's like there's not a doubt in his mind that Jake's the one who killed her. I feel like I'm going to be sick.

"Half this town drives black trucks, including your son," I point out.

"My son's never been in that neighborhood before, I assure you."

The ignorance of the statement is overwhelming, yet he doesn't seem to realize it. And the deputy behind him just nods along like a bobblehead, backing him up.

"I suppose there's not much more I can do right now if y'all are sticking to your story. But if either of you decide you have something to say about what happened to that poor girl, you know where to find me."

Though the sheriff addresses us both, his eyes are on me, boring a hole through my flesh like he can see the doubt beneath. I hold my breath, refusing to let myself look away until, with a weary sigh, he tells his deputy to meet him back at the station.

Though Jed can't seem to get out of here fast enough, Sheriff Kingston takes his time returning to his vehicle like he's trying to give me a chance to change my mind. Even after he closes the cruiser door and starts the engine, he lingers. I can feel him studying me through the darkly tinted window.

Finally, he puts his car in gear. I watch as he makes a small circle in the yard before driving away, not sure if I want him to stop and stay. Not sure what I trust, or who.

Ten minutes ago, I would have said that there was no way Jake was a murderer, despite his other faults, but now? If the sheriff's right, the dead woman was strangled. And if I'm right, so was Butch.

CHAPTER 15

The instant Sheriff Kingston's cruiser disappears from sight, Jake takes a seat on the bottom rail of the fence, landing heavily, his head in his hands. I listen to the ragged, labored sounds of his breathing. Study his posture, the way his broad shoulders have folded in on themselves, his body suddenly seeming half the size it once was.

Jake isn't an idiot. He couldn't have known that I'd give him an alibi. But could he have anticipated that his truck would be seen during the dark hours of the morning?

In this area? Yes.

Maybe there's money to be made in the surrounding towns, but here in the swamp, people are forced to do whatever they can to put food on the table. Fishing, frog gigging, and gator hunting are best done under the cover of darkness. There's just as much traffic, as sparse as it is, around here at 3:00 a.m. as at 3:00 p.m.

But do I trust him? I'm not sure. To be fair, I'm not sure if I trust any man right now. But Butch trusted him. And I trusted Butch.

I'm still trying to work out what that means when Jake stands, the sudden movement drawing my attention. He looks at me with reddened eyes. "You shouldn't have done that."

"Done what?"

"Lied to Kingston. Given me an alibi."

"I didn't lie," I say, swallowing hard. "I never confirmed that you were here all night. Just that you were helping me."

"That's not the way he saw it."

"It's not my problem what he sees."

"Unless other law enforcement gets brought in on the investigation, which they just might. And if they do, they're going to be asking you that same question."

And if that happens, I'm going to have to tell the truth. The full truth because evasive statements aren't going to work on a real detective. I pull at my shirt collar, a flush creeping up my neck at the thought of what that might mean.

Jake's gaze sharpens on my face. I find myself looking away from the searing intensity. "What's wrong? You don't think I had anything to do with it, do you?"

"Of course not."

His face crumples. "But?"

I rub my lips together as I shake my head, trying to think of the best way to sensitively broach what I need to say.

"Where did Grace live?" I finally ask.

"The Sugarcane District. Why?"

I hear the sharp hiss of my breath, can feel that my eyes are open too wide, my heart picking up its tempo inside my chest.

"What aren't you telling me?" he asks.

The Sugarcane District is one of the few neighborhoods that exist out here in the swamp, the houses built on land that used to be part of an old sugarcane plantation that folded in the late 1800s and sat abandoned until it was developed in the 1960s. And it's close.

So close, in fact, that several of the properties back up to the sanctuary, past the woods on the far side of Chomp's pond. Any doubts I had about whether there is a link between the two deaths have been erased. Now it seems unlikely that there isn't a connection.

Is it possible that what happened to Butch wasn't because of who he was, but because of where he was?

I need to say something, gauge Jake's reaction.

"Yesterday, at the viewing," I begin. "I noticed something strange."

"About the funeral?"

"About Butch."

His eyes flash the same way Daisy's had last night—with the wariness of a wild animal.

"There was a mark around his neck. Bruising."

"I didn't see any bruising."

"It was under his shirt collar. I only noticed because I knew he would hate being so constricted, so I unbuttoned it."

Jake keeps staring at me with something bordering on disbelief.

"No," he says. "I mean when I found him. He was wearing a T-shirt. When I laid him down to give him CPR, I would have noticed."

"Wait. You're the one who found him?"

His Adam's apple bulges as he swallows hard, but his gaze never leaves mine as he says, "Yes."

"Was he still warm?"

"Yes. That's why I started CPR as soon as I'd called for an ambulance. I tried. You have to believe me. I did everything I could, but…"

"Jake, do you remember seeing anyone else that day? Did you pass any vehicles on your way here?"
"I don't know. I wasn't paying attention. Why?"

"Because if you didn't see a bruise, then it's

possible it hadn't appeared yet."

"Can that happen?"

"Yes. If Butch had just been killed—"

"You can't stay here."

"I'm not going anywhere until I find whoever's responsible—"

"I'm not saying leave the area. But you can't stay here at the sanctuary. Not by yourself."

The look I give him makes him curse. He runs his hands through his hair, pacing.

"You need new doors for the house. I'll call around, see if I can find some in stock. If not, I'll get some ordered. This is all my fault. I tried to get Butch to change them or at least let me install some better locks. I'm sorry, Cassie. I should have tried harder."

"Why did you think Butch needed extra security?"

Jake grimaces. "I'd noticed strange tire marks on the property in areas where neither Butch nor I drove. And he started mentioning things that had gone missing around the house."

"Was his memory going?"

"Not that I could tell. His hearing, yes, and his vision—"

"Wait, what?"

Tears well in my eyes as I wait for him to answer. His surprise morphs into sympathy.

"You really didn't know, did you?"

I shake my head, unable to trust myself to speak just yet.

He curses again. "He promised me he'd tell you."

"Well, he didn't."

Jake's tone is gentle as he says, "He could still see well enough to get around, but he'd lost so much of his central vision that he was legally blind. I drove him to all his appointments. The doctor couldn't say how fast the macular degeneration would progress, or even if it would. Just that there was no regaining the vision that had already been lost."

"So when he canceled his visit a couple of months ago… he told me it was because he'd taken in an emergency foster." This time, I'm the one to curse. "I knew he was lying. I knew but I didn't press him. I figured he just didn't feel like making the trip. I should have asked him what was really going on. Maybe if I had—"

"It's not your fault."

"Isn't it? Butch needed me. I should have been here."

"It's not. No more than it's mine for not picking him up and carrying him out of here against his will. You of all people know how stubborn he was. It appears to be a hereditary trait."

I ignore the jab—and the unimplied threat that he should carry me out of here against my will—and instead ask, "If you thought there was a threat, why didn't you tell me? Why am I just learning about this now?"

Jake looks at the ground, digging the toe of one steel toe boot into the dirt as he says, "Because I figured you had a gun. And because I wasn't sure, not enough to make you worry like that. Butch was getting older. It wasn't impossible that he forgot where he put something or chose to drive out to inspect the fences instead of walk and just didn't want to admit it. And… I was afraid you'd hate me."

"Huh?"

"When I found him like that, it made me really think about all the things he did around here. I mean, how many people are still doing hard labor at his age? I should have known better. Done more for him. Made him take it easy."

"We both know that wouldn't have worked."

"But I could have tried."

"Was he under treatment for a heart condition?"

"Not that I know of."

"How long had you been taking him to his doctor appointments?"

"Five, maybe six months."

"There's something more going on here," I say. "His death certificate was signed off on. That's why an autopsy wasn't performed. But if there was no attending physician for a preexisting heart issue, then there's no way that should have happened."

"When will you know what his cause of death was for sure?"

I shrug. "Tomorrow's the first weekday since the viewing. I don't know how backlogged the ME's office is, but hopefully soon."

"Not soon enough," Jake mutters as the sound of an engine carries down the drive. He takes a step closer to me as a black truck much like his own appears, the air between us so still that I think we both must be holding our breath as the vehicle rolls to a stop before us.

I exhale noisily as the door opens and Gordon's face appears.

"Hey, Cassidy." He gives a small wave, casting a dubious look between me and Jake, as if he knows he's interrupting something. "We never got a chance to say goodbye yesterday. I wanted to check and make sure you're doing okay."

"Yeah, sorry. Everything's fine."

"You sure?"

This time the look he gives Jake is downright suspicious.

"Yes."

"I don't suppose you could spare a few minutes for an old friend? And maybe a cold drink?"

"Sure. Let's go inside."

He nods, then starts toward the house.

"You coming?" I ask Jake.

"That's one of your friends from school, right?"

"Mmhmm, Gordon Massey."

"Do you feel comfortable being alone with him?"

"Yes."

"Then I'll stay out here. There are a few things I want to check real quick. But Cassie?" I stop, turning back to look at him. "Be careful, okay?"

"Of course."

I give him a smile though it's the second to last thing I want to do. Then I head inside to speak with my old friend, which is the first.

Because I'm not the girl I used to be. I'm nothing like her. And the only way I'll know for sure whether that's a bad thing or not is by talking to the friends who used to know me.

CHAPTER 16

I pretend not to notice Gordon try the doorknob, or the odd look he gives me when I pull my keys out and unlock the door. I know that Butch never bothered with locks. It's part of the reason the word animal was never used in any of the wording for this place, the name of the farm simply Gator Glade Sanctuary—because he wanted it to be a safe place for all creatures, humans included.

It wasn't abnormal for me to come home from an after-school activity to find friends, or even enemies, inside watching TV, cooking, making themselves at home. Butch welcomed them all. It's one of the things that endeared him to the community. Now it seems possible that it might have been his downfall, as well.

I try not to dwell on the dark thoughts lurking in the shadows of my mind, instead turning to Gordon with the brightest smile I can muster. "So. What can I get you to drink?"

"Actually, I'm good. I just wanted a chance to talk to you alone."

"What about?"

He makes a face, then turns away, heading toward the kitchen. I trail after him, waiting for an answer.

"Was that Jake Walker? I didn't know you knew him."

"Yeah, we go way back. Our moms were best friends."

"Cass, that was a long time ago. People change."

"And?"

"And you shouldn't trust someone just because you used to know them."

I arch my eyebrows at him. "By that logic, I shouldn't trust you either."

He breaks out into a wide grin. "But you will, because I'm still the same old Gordo. I haven't changed at all."

"Uh, not true. You're barely recognizable."

"That's just because decades of lifting weights finally paid off and I'm no longer thinner than a piece of straw. But in all the ways that count, I'm the same me."

"If you say so."

His smile falters. I grab the dishtowel off the counter and give it a wipe even though it's already clean. My skin bristles as he takes a closer look at me.

"I really am sorry about Butch. He was a great guy."

I nod, not trusting my voice enough to speak.

"Have you given any thought about what you're going to do? I mean, this place is all yours now, right?"

He taps a finger on the stack of papers on the table. I feel a surge of annoyance, wanting to sweep the envelope from Myers and Kleinman away from where he can see it. Wishing I'd had the foresight to hide it from prying eyes, but I hadn't expected to invite anyone inside, and I needed the visual reminder—I'm still trying to work up my nerve to read what's inside.

"For my sake, I hope you decide to stick around, but if you do decide to leave, I have a developer friend who would kill for this property."

I give him a sharp look. I realize it's just a phrase

of speech, but it hit a raw spot.

"I mean, even if you want to keep the sanctuary going," Gordon says, not seeming to notice my discomfort, "I bet you could get him to build you a bigger, better barn and a new house on another piece of land as part of the deal."

"Why?" I ask.

"Why what?"

"Why would he kill for this property?"

Gordon gives me a blank look, but I can see the wheels spinning behind his neutral expression. And it's taking him too long to answer.

Suspicion jabs at my skin like a million needle pricks. I realize that I'm probably blowing something he randomly said out of proportion, but I need an answer. Because what if someone really would kill for this property?

"There are thousands of acres just waiting to be developed around here. What makes this land so special?" I prod.

Something flashes behind his eyes that I don't like, a mirror of my own annoyance from a moment ago. The difference is, I noticed. I cross my arms, narrowing my gaze as the discomfort in the room grows.

"I was just making conversation," he finally says.

"Were you? What if I said I wanted to speak with this developer friend of yours? Sell him the land?"

"Then he would probably buy the property if you offered it to him as a favor to me, because we," he gestures between us, "are friends. And it's already mostly cleared and has good road frontage, which are two things he's always talking about looking for."

"So, the whole building a new barn and house as part of the deal?"

His jaw tenses, a muscle ticking in his cheek. "I

may have gotten ahead of myself."

Gordon looks at me like he expects a reply. Or maybe an apology. But he's not going to get either. I can't quite put my finger on what it is, but something stinks.

"Well, like I said, I just wanted to stop by and check on how you're doing after you left Butch's funeral so suddenly yesterday. I'm glad to see you're well."

Am I being paranoid, or was there a note of sarcasm in his voice?

"Anyway, I'll let you get back to *whatever* it was you were doing." There's no mistaking the scorn in his tone this time. "I'll see you around."

I follow him to the door, stand there watching as he walks to his truck and climbs inside. As he starts the vehicle, a cloud of exhaust spitting from the tailpipe. As he drives back toward the road in a haze of dust.

It's not until he disappears from sight that I step back inside and close the door. Studying it, I wonder how to make it more secure. In fact, the whole house needs to be checked. I need to do whatever I can to make this place safer. Because the only thing I trust right now is my gut.

Something strange is going on here. And I'm worried that whatever it is, it's just getting started.

CHAPTER 17

I'm in the barn cleaning when I hear the rumble of an engine approaching. Adrenaline spreads beneath my skin, making it feel too tight. My flesh ripples as goosebumps rise. I was alone at the sanctuary. But I'm not anymore.

It's only been twenty minutes since Jake left to get something he needed from the hardware store. He hasn't even had time to get there yet. Which means whoever this is, it's not someone I'm expecting.

I duck down beneath the window in Chip and Bagel's stall, one of the pigs—I still haven't learned to tell them apart—sliming my hand with his muddy snout as I watch to see who's coming. Though I don't recognize the vehicle, a battered forest green pickup with a camper on back, at least the truck isn't black, which is a start.

A grey-haired man wearing glasses emerges a moment later. Though he looks harmless enough, I grab the pitchfork I'd been using and bring it with me as I go to see what he wants. He waves when he spots me, closing the distance between us with a confident stride.

"I don't believe we've met before. I'm Dr. Craig Vincent. Heard you have a baby zebra for me to look at."

It's the vet. The relief I feel is so overwhelming that I want to cry.

"I'm Butch's granddaughter, Cassidy. Pleased to meet you." I reach to accept his offer of a handshake. Catch sight of the smear across my palm and offer a smile instead. "Sorry. One of the pigs got me."

He takes my hand anyway, giving it an exuberant pump up and down accompanied by a friendly grin. "It's nothing I'm not used to. Now. Where's the little one?"

"In the barn."

He falls into step beside me, though I assume he knows the way.

"Did Daisy have any trouble with the delivery?"

"The foal was breech. I had to turn her around."

He turns and squints at me through his glasses. It gives him an owlish appearance.

"They're both fine now?"

"They appear to be."

"You ever do something like that before?"

Shaking my head, I admit, "No. I haven't even witnessed a birth in over two decades."

"You said you're Butch's granddaughter?"

"Yes."

"Didn't know he had one of those."

It feels like I've been punched in the gut. "I've been away for a while."

"Oh yeah? Where at?"

"Virginia," I say, being purposely vague.

"Pretty up there."

"It is."

"Here they are," he says, addressing Daisy and the foal like old friends. Letting himself into the stall, he croons to the zebra, "I bet you're happy to have that baby out, aren't you?"

Glancing at me, he adds, "And I bet Jake's glad he gets to stop camping out every night. Not that the company's not good." He gives the mare an affectionate rub behind the ear. "Where is he, anyway?"

"Jake?"

"The way he's been blowing up my phone the last week, I would have expected him to be here."

I don't respond, instead watching as he runs his hands over the foal, looking into her eyes, checking her gums. When he's done, he rests his arms along the top of the stall door. Though I can feel him studying me, I pretend not to notice.

"I was sorry to hear about Butch. He was one of the good ones. One of the best."

"Thank you."

"Jake, too."

"Butch relied on him a lot, didn't he?"

"More so over the last few years, but yeah, I'd say that's pretty accurate."

"So he trusted him, then?"

Dr. Vincent cranes his head forward as he takes a closer look at me. "I get the feeling there's something you want to ask."

"Jake and I grew up together, but I've been gone a long time. I don't want to… burden him by asking too much."

"As far as these animals are concerned, I don't think there's an ask that could be too big. Jake loves them every bit as much as your grandfather did." He gives me a sympathetic frown. "Why don't you tell me what's got you so worried? We'll see if I can't help."

I lick my lips, trying to decide what to say. Butch trusted Jake. As strange as it feels, *I* trust Jake. I think.

Either way, I shouldn't be running my mouth about murdered ex-girlfriends and neighbors who think they saw Jake's truck at the scene of the crime. But I've backed myself into a corner. I have to come up with some kind of an explanation for my questions, one other than that I'm trying to make myself feel less like the stupid girl in a horror movie who believes someone just because she's attracted to them.

I settle on, "It's nothing really. It's just, I came home from Butch's funeral yesterday and found some guy with a horse trailer here. He was planning on taking them." I gesture toward the zebras.

"You catch this guy's name?"

"Jeff Gates."

Dr. Vincent curses under his breath. "That guy is a total nightmare."

"Had he been giving Butch a hard time?"

"Not that I know of, but your grandfather wouldn't have necessarily told me if he was. But what I can tell you is that he's the absolute last person Butch would have trusted with their care."

"Yeah, I recognized the name."

"Were you worried about asking Jake to help you keep an eye on them?"

I wasn't, but there's no way I can tell him what I'm really worried about, so I nod. "I didn't want to impose."

"Honestly? I wouldn't worry about that. You asked me if your grandfather trusted Jake. I'd have to say that, present company excluded, there was no one he trusted more. Butch had a big heart, but he wasn't a fool. That old man was an excellent judge of character. No matter how much he wanted to see the best in everyone, his eyes were wide open to the truth, no matter how hard it was to face."

I wish I was more like Butch. Instead, it's quite possible that we were opposites. Forcing a swallow past the lump in my throat, I say, "Thank you."

"Now then. That is one good-looking baby zebra you have on your hands. Any idea what you're going to name her?"

I haven't given it any thought, but the answer seems obvious. She should be named after the man who did everything he could to give her a safe home. I think Butch would like that.

"Charlie," I say.

The vet nods his approval with a sad smile.

"As far as I can tell, both these girls are in perfect health. Is there anyone else I need to take a look at while I'm here?"

I smile as I shake my head, blinking back tears. As much of a relief as it is to know that Butch trusted Jake, and that the zebras are healthy, there's one thing that the vet got wrong. My grandfather was an excellent judge of character—but I don't think he trusted me at all. Why else would he have kept so much about what was going on hidden from me?

CHAPTER 18

You'd think that summertime would be peak season here in Gator Glade, but it's not. It's too hot and humid for the tourists—and their money. Because of that, two-thirds of the town shuts down during the off season, which is fine, if you're prepared for it.

I'm not.

I need a drink. Not a binge like last night, just something to help me relax enough to get my shoulders down from around my ears, and maybe a few hours of sleep. But I dropped the bottle I'd been drinking from last night in my haste to get to Daisy. I can't find any other alcohol in the house. And the small liquor store at the back of the gift shop in town is closed on Sundays.

Which is why I decide to visit the Gladesman's Fish and Game Club, the town's only year-round bar. It's not like half of Gator Glade doesn't know I'm back by now. Or like it will do any use to stay in hiding.

Only… first I have to figure out how to escape. I park in front of the barrier Jake jerry rigged, an ancient metal gate piece that had been rusting in the grass now stretched across the driveway, each end chained around a tree and padlocked.

It was supposed to make me feel more secure. Instead, it's made me feel trapped. But desperation is a powerful motivator, and that's exactly what I am, standing here getting eaten alive by mosquitoes.

I pick an end to unlock, grunting and groaning as I drag it until there's a big enough gap for me to drive through. I move my car to the other side, then get out and repeat the process. I'd love to leave it open. If I do manage to relax and unwind a bit, the moment I get back and have to do this again, it will all be undone . But what if I don't lock it and something bad happens while I'm gone? Like a zebra theft?

Getting back in my car, I take a moment to catch my breath, to scrub the rust stains from my palms with hand sanitizer and Starbucks napkins that crumble as soon as they get wet, then I'm on my way. The drive isn't long enough for my anxiety to grow too overwhelming, but it doesn't matter. The instant I pull into the only empty spot left in the packed parking lot, my nerves skyrocket.

I tell myself it will be all right as I cross the cracked tarmac, pausing with my hand on the door. I've never been inside before. I was too young when I left, but I'd heard plenty of rumors about what it was like, none of them very flattering.

But really—how bad can it be? Pushing the door open, I step over the threshold and find my breath sucked away by the answer.

It's worse than I was led to believe. Much worse.

Dark wood paneling drains the light from the room, but even the dimness can't conceal how filthy it is. It reeks of stale beer, which would explain why my shoes stick like Velcro to the floor, but there's something worse hiding underneath the stench that makes my nose drip and my toes curl.

High shelves line the walls, every one of them crammed full of taxidermied animals. Not just your average deer, turkey, and raccoons, but black bears, bobcats, otters, even a flamingo. It's like I had a nightmare that threw up on my reality.

Squaring my shoulders, I force myself farther inside, pretending not to notice the attention I draw as I cross the room and take a seat on a stool at the counter. Not so stealthy whispers carry to my ears as I order. I promise myself I'll leave after one drink, wishing I'd found some lead paint to chug at home instead of coming here tonight.

Though I'm eager to leave as soon as possible, I force myself to sip slowly, not wanting to give these people anything else to gossip about. I'm holding my breath, listening to a particularly unflattering explanation about how I've been gone for the last two decades because I've been in prison, when someone slides onto the stool beside me.

"Hey, I remember you."

I lift my eyes to find Alicia Harris smiling at me. She'd been a couple years ahead of me in school. I don't think we've ever talked before. She'd been too cool, and I'd been too young. But time is a great equalizer.

"I remember you, too."

"Sorry about your grandfather," she says.

"Did you know him?" I ask, genuinely curious as to how their paths had crossed.

"No. I never met him, actually. But anybody who loved animals as much as he did has to be a good person, right?"

I smile, unsure how to answer.

"FYI, you're going to be a hot commodity, now that you're back."

"How's that?"

"New blood. Even though you're not really new, I guess, but you're close enough. You know how incestuous this place is. All the eligible bachelors are going to be all over you. And between us girls?" She looks around, checking to see who's nearby before leaning her head close to mine and announcing in a loud stage whisper, "They're all eligible because no woman in their right mind would want them."

We share a laugh, and I'm surprised at how good it feels. How genuine. How much like something that's been missing from my life for way too long.

"Cute purse," I say, gesturing to the oversized black leather bag she set on the counter between us, the accents and adjustable slider on the strap a unique antique pewter color.

"Thanks," she beams. "So, what have you been up to all these years?"

"Oh, you know. First there was school, then there was work, followed by more work, which led to me selling my soul in the hopes that the job wouldn't be a dead end."

"But the devil has a sense of humor and sent you back to Gator Glade to put hell into perspective, so you'd work longer hours for less pay?"

"Something like that," I grin.

She returns it, then rolls her eyes as a man behind us loudly airs his opinion about why I supposedly spent the last twenty years incarcerated.

"Hey, Rodger?" Alicia yells over her shoulder. "You're wrong. She hasn't been in prison all this time, she's been the lead recruiter for a cannibalistic doomsday cult, so you better shut up unless you want to be on the menu."

"Really?"

"No, not really!" she says, turning to look at him. "Good grief. What's wrong with you?"

"Sorry."

"You should be." She spins back toward me and

grimaces. "Sorry about that. Hey, listen. Why don't we get out of here? You shouldn't have to deal with this crap, especially right now. I have a brand-new bottle of tequila at my place."

"Oh. Thank you, but I really should be getting home now."

"Then I'll bring it to your place. I live right down the road. It'll take me less than two minutes to grab it. I know where the sanctuary is. Go on and start, I'll catch up with you."

I can't think of a polite excuse, and if I'm being honest, I'm not sure I want to. The house has felt so empty, especially at night. Maybe company is what I'm really after, not the drink. Alicia's watching me closely with a hopeful look on her face.

"Okay," I say. "Sure."

"Great! I'll see you there."

I settle my bill and head out to the parking lot. Get in my car, taking my time as I strap myself in and start the engine, wondering if I've made the right decision. If I remember correctly, Alicia wasn't the nicest person when we were in school.

But people change. They mature. Evolve. Do better. Besides, what's the worst that will happen? I decide not to invite her back?

I pull up to the single stoplight, the one that leads out of town, and turn onto the vacant stretch of road that will take me home. Flick on my brights, eyes peeled. It's a lesson you learn young out here in the middle of nowhere—to drive carefully, especially at night. You never know what's sharing the dark with you.

My hands curl tighter around the steering wheel as a shudder runs through me. Though I'd been thinking about animals, as I pass the turnoff for the neighborhood where Grace Billie lived, another type of predator comes to mind.

It's a relief when headlights appear in the distance behind me. But are we any safer when we're not alone? Grace lived in a residential area. Her neighbors noticed a truck parked outside her house. But her proximity to civilization did nothing to protect her.

The vehicle behind me is closer now, approaching much too quickly. I feel a surge of anger at the carelessness of the driver. The feeling morphs into something else as they close the distance between us, a dark truck now distinguishable against the backdrop of night, and I find myself pushing my own speed faster.

CHAPTER 19

My breath catches, heart pounding as I glance at my speedometer, the needle creeping higher and higher still, yet the distance between my car and the truck behind me continues to shrink. I'll have to slow down soon. The driveway for the sanctuary is just up ahead.

Or should I keep going?

No. I'll be safer on my own turf.

I shift my weight, leaning forward in my seat, watching the trees for the telltale flash of the reflectors Butch attached to them when I first started driving so I'd be able to find the turn at night. Spotting the trio of orange plastic beacons, I put on my turn signal and take my foot off the gas.

I'd been hoping that when the other driver realized I was going to brake, they'd zip by me in the other lane, the way I've been passed so many times before in this very spot. Instead, they stay right on my tail as I slow, coming to a near stop before making the turn off the main road. Then jerking to a sudden halt as my headlights illuminate the gate Jake had rigged.

The truck pulls over onto the shoulder right behind me. I stare at it in my rearview, trying to make out the person, but it's too dark. Their head is just a shadow behind the wheel.

Anxiety floods through me in giant crashing

waves, tsunamis of fear sweeping me up in their embrace. If only they could carry me to safety. Instead, I feel the air being sucked from my lungs. My head spins.

I blink, the darkness, the night, the woods momentarily being replaced by a musty basement, the dirt floor cold and hard beneath me, the handcuffs that trap my hands behind my back biting deep into my flesh. Another blink, and my true surroundings reappear.

A plan forms in my mind. Climb over the fence. Hide among the trees. Make my way to the house and ransack the place until I find Butch's gun. Because there's another monster to escape from, and this time, I don't have the element of surprise in my favor.

I need to get out of here.

Unbuckling my seatbelt, I kick the door open, leaving the car running as I jump out and run for the fence. Behind me, I hear the creak of another door. The dull thud of another set of feet hitting the ground. I'm almost to the fence when a voice cracks through the night, so sudden and unexpected that even the frogs fall silent.

"Boy, am I glad that I managed to catch up with you! There's no way I would have found the driveway. It is *dark* out here, isn't it?"

I turn toward Alicia, feeling like an idiot. Hoping she can't see how badly I'm shaking.

"I'll have the gate open in just a second. You can wait in your car if you want, away from the mosquitoes."

"Great, thanks."

As soon as I hear her door close, I can breathe again. It takes me several tries to fit the key in the lock, but once I have it open, I drag the gate out of the way in no time using pure adrenaline. Decide to leave it open so I won't have to deal with it again tonight when Alicia leaves.

By the time I've gotten back in my car and led the way up to the house, I feel like I can pass as some semblance of normal, which seems confirmed as Alicia gives me a wide smile, apparently not having picked up on my meltdown, as I hold the front door open for her.

"Is that gate new? I don't remember seeing it before," she says as I usher her toward the kitchen.

"Yeah. Jake just set it up earlier today."

"Jake? Wait. You don't mean Jake Walker, do you?"

"Yeah," I say, pulling a couple of glasses from the cabinet.

"Dang, girl. I've got to hand it to you. I didn't even know he was still around, but you've been back less than a week and you've already found the hottest guy to ever attend Glade High and got him busy building you a fortress. Has he lost his hair and gained a beer belly yet?"

I shake my head. "He's done that incredibly unfair thing guys do when they get better looking with age."

"Ugh. I feel like I should hate you," she says, but there's no animosity in the grin she's giving me. "But since we're friends now, I expect all the juicy details instead."

My cheeks burn as I watch her pour two fingers of tequila in each glass. I chose the smallest cups I could find, but it's still a lot of alcohol.

"It's not like that," I say.

"It sure looks like it is. That gate looked heavy AF. There's not many men who would have done that for me if I asked them."

"I didn't ask him."

"Okay, now I know there's more going on than you're telling me."

That familiar band tightens around my chest. I

rub the back of my neck, my hairline damp with sweat. I'm not sure what to tell her, but I know I should say something. I should warn her. She needs to know that there's a killer on the loose so she can be more careful.

"A woman who lived in the old Sugarcane District neighborhood was murdered last night. Grace Billie."

I take a deep breath, intending to continue, but I can't seem to make the words come out—the ones that would lump Butch into what's going on.

"Wow, seriously?"

"Yes."

"You're braver than I am, staying out here all by yourself after something like that happened so close. I'd have hightailed it out of here, called a real estate agent to sell the place from the road and never looked back. No wonder you needed a drink."

I look at her over the rim of my glass, taking a long sip in response.

"But, I mean, come on. That still doesn't explain why Jake Walker just decided to put that thing up on his own."

I shrug. "We've been friends since we were little."

"And?"

"And there's been some slimeball lurking around, trying to take a zebra Butch rescued."

Her mouth drops open. "You have a zebra?"

"Two. She just gave birth."

"A baby zebra," she squeals. "Tell me it's okay for me to come back in the daylight some time so I can see it?"

"Yeah, of course it is."

"Yay."

She reaches across the table to pour me a refill. I

stare at the glass, not having realized it was empty already. Slide my gaze over to her drink, which appears untouched.

"So Jake built the fence because he's in love with the zebra, not you?"

"Something like that, yeah."

"Mmhmm." She gives me a knowing smile. "And nothing's happened between you two?"

"No."

I work hard to keep my expression blank, to not betray my lie. Because something has happened between me and Jake, I just haven't been able to label what it is yet. And until I can, there's no use complicating an already thorny matter.

"Good. Because the last thing you need is to get trapped in Gator Glade." She tosses back her drink. "Don't get me wrong. I'd love it if you stuck around. I mean, yeah, we don't know each other very well, but you made it out of here, which already makes you more interesting than every other person here."

Alicia studies me as she refills her glass. It feels like she's peeling back the layers of my skin, looking at the secrets hidden beneath.

"My point is, you made it out once. And you know what they say—lightning doesn't strike the same place twice. My advice is to get out of here as soon as you can. And to take me with you," she adds with a wink. "What plans has your grandfather made for this place?"

My eyes slide involuntarily to the thick envelope from Myers and Kleinman that remains unopened in the center of the table as I mutter, "I don't know."

"What do you mean, you don't know?"

Following my gaze, she reaches toward the package. Though I know I should stop her, I don't. Maybe I can't. Or maybe it's that I need to hear what she has to say. She drags it closer to her and flips it over. Gives me a questioning look.

"Is this what I think it is?" she asks. "Is this your grandfather's will?"

I stare down at the glass in my hands, somehow empty again already.

"It hasn't even been opened. Please tell me that this is just a copy? That you already know what it says?"

I tuck my lips inside my mouth to keep them from trembling.

"Oh," she says quietly. Then louder, "Hey, don't cry."

Her fingers are cool and soft as she pats my hand. As she flips it over, palm up, and sets the envelope on top. "But this isn't something you can put off forever. My advice is to pull the Band-Aid off quickly and get it over with. Then do what you need to do and get out of here while you still have the chance."

Alicia stands, grabbing my phone from the table. She holds it in front of my face until the screen unlocks, then types quickly with her thumbs. A moment later, a buzz sounds from her purse.

"There, now you have my number."

"You're leaving?" I feel a jolt of panic, not wanting to be alone just yet.

"I've got an early morning tomorrow. And you've got something you need to do."

She gives my shoulder a light squeeze, then she's gone, the door shutting gently behind her. I know I should get up and lock it, but I remain frozen, staring at the envelope in my hand instead.

I know she's right. This is exactly what I needed—an impartial third party to act as a sounding board. Someone I can trust. Which means someone who doesn't have anything to gain from manipulating me.

Grabbing the corner of the flap, I pull, tearing the package open.

CHAPTER 20

My hands shake as I upend the envelope, causing the papers inside to fall out onto the table. I study them where they land, looking for some hidden danger—a sharp object, a poisonous powder, a lethal snake—but there's nothing more ominous than the law firm's logo printed boldly on the cover letter that tops the stack.

The page is cream-colored, thick, high quality. Everything about it, from the swanky Marco Island address to the embossed design, screams expensive. I check my phone, knowing that no alerts have come in during the last few minutes, that none of the ones I'm waiting for will arrive until tomorrow at the soonest, yet I allow myself the distraction, because I'm once again left wondering exactly what Butch's connection to these people was.

Because my grandfather's distaste for lawyers, especially the kind who wield money and power like these ones, makes this alliance he somehow formed with them seem like the most unlikely thing I've uncovered since I've been back. It just doesn't add up. Leopards don't change their spots, and this… it feels an awful lot like circles being called stripes.

Typing Myers and Kleinman into the search bar on my screen, I wait for the results to load, once again clicking on the law firm's website. I take my time exploring each page, looking for something to help this make sense, but if anything, it just makes my frustration grow.

I'd been hoping to spot someone I recognized, or that I at least could imagine Butch having known. Instead, I find that besides the names of the founding partners, there's not one employee identified. That can't be normal.

Out of curiosity, I visit websites for several other law offices. As expected, each one has brief bios about the attorneys who work there, tidbits about their education, their experience, and their achievements. The kind of information that would help you make the decision about who to hire.

So why is Myers and Kleinman different? How do they get new clients? Does all their business come from word of mouth? Or do they not care about things like that? And if that's the case, how do they make money? Suspicion coats my tongue with a bitter taste.

Thankfully, tomorrow's Monday. As long as she shows up for work, Mallory Chan will see the email I sent her asking for information. With an ounce of luck, she'll be able to get me the details I need to fill in the blanks. Because the only thing I know for sure right now is that there's too much that I don't know.

I assure myself that one way or another, this mystery will be revealed as I turn my attention to the cover letter. It's standard generic fare, nothing to even suggest that whoever wrote it knew anything more about Butch than his legal name and that his payment cleared. It's exactly the type of thing he would hate.

Setting it aside, I reach for the stack, bound together by a big clip at the top. Tears gather in my eyes as I read through the legalese, a convoluted collection of words that take way too long to say one simple thing—

he's left everything to me. It's what I expected, only now that it's confirmed, the weight of the choices I'm forced to make, the futures left up to me to decide, settle heavily on my back.

It's why I put this off for as long as I could. Butch loved this place. What it stood for. What he accomplished here. Every animal that set paw, hoof, talon, or foot on this land became a part of him, a piece of his heart. And now what happens to them is up to me.

Butch was well known among the animal rescues in the state. Chances are good that they'd come together and help me find new homes for everyone. Despite that, I'm hesitant to ask for their help.

Because someone who is great with reptiles might be horrible with avians. Likewise, some people who are wonderful with small animals might be terrible with large ones. And you can't pick and choose when someone's doing you a favor.

I know that Butch had very strong opinions about this kind of thing. I just wish I knew exactly what he'd want me to do.

Reaching the end of the document, I find two envelopes paperclipped to the last page. One has my name written on it. The other is taped shut and bears the instruction: READ LAST.

Something inside my stomach shifts, distant memories mixed with longing. Whatever doubts I might have about my grandfather's relationship with Myers and Kleinman, this is very much a Butch move.

Like I said, he had strong opinions. And I suspect I'm going to get my wish. He's done me one final favor. He's letting me know what to do.

I suck in a deep, ragged breath and open the envelope with my name written on it. Pull out the letter inside, the words on it, written in Butch's barely legible scrawl, blurring through the tears that film my eyes. Wiping them away, I read:

Butch didn't know. He couldn't have. Because there's no way he'd have left this note for me if he'd been aware that his life was in danger, not if he even suspected it.

Which means that either his murder was random, or that whoever killed him was a part of his life, just waiting until they found the right moment to strike. And people like that, the kind who smile at you even as they slide the knife into your gut, slicing deep, are the most dangerous kind.

CHAPTER 21

I keep the phone clenched tightly in my hand though my knuckles throb and my tendons spasm and twitch. Press the device so firmly against my ear that it aches. But the physical pain is nothing compared to the anguish waging a war inside me, filling my body to the brim with the need to find answers.

The ringing stops, and for a moment, I worry that I'll be forced to continue to wait. To dial again, and again, and again, the way I've been doing all morning. But then I hear something shift on the other end of the line, an intake or expulsion of air, and I draw a deep breath of my own, steeling myself for the task at hand.

"Rich Bailey, here."

"Yes, hi, it's Special Agent Cassidy Knox. We met this weekend at—" My voice cracks.

"Yes, Agent Knox, I remember. What can I help you with?"

"A body was discovered this weekend. A local woman, Grace Billie."

The grunt he responds with sets my teeth on edge.

"Sheriff Kingston told me she was strangled."

"He did?"

The surprise in his tone is unmistakable. I don't confide that it wasn't in an official capacity. That the sheriff doesn't even know my connection to law enforcement. I'll take whatever advantage I can muster and deal with the consequences later.

"He did. I'm calling because I wanted to ask—was she manually strangulated? Or was a ligature used?"

The line falls so silent that I hold my breath in fear of missing his answer. Finally, he says, "This isn't something we should be discussing. Not unless you're offering your services in a professional capacity."

"I am." The words gush out on that held breath, too loud and forceful. I keep speaking anyway, afraid to give myself the chance to think. "I'll help in any way I can. Anything you need."

"I appreciate that," he says slowly. "But I'm afraid I must decline."

My fingers curl even tighter around the phone until my knuckles feel like they're going to burst. Disappointment causes the pressure in the room around me to shift, to squeeze around me like a snake constricting its prey. I prepare myself to be swallowed whole as I wait for his rejection to continue.

The man clears his throat. I hear the suction of a door opening. The click of it closing. His voice is low as he says, "It would be inappropriate for you to assist on a case that so closely mirrors your grandfather's."

I gasp, faltering the phone which I'd done such a good job of holding until now. I fumble it against the side of my head, heart drumming so loudly that I almost can't hear myself speak as I fire off questions.

"How similar are they? Was the same type of ligature used? Can I come in and view her bruises myself?"

"I'm afraid that's not possible. I'm sure you can appreciate the delicate nature of the situation, Agent Knox. I've asked that your grandfather's postmortem be completed as soon as possible for that very reason. In the meantime, you should know that a detective has already been assigned to the case—Miguel Torres."

I yank open drawers in the kitchen until I find a pen. Scribble the name on the envelope Butch's water bill arrived in.

"Miguel and I go way back," he continues. "Rest assured that the case is in good hands. And I'm sure he'll be in contact as soon as we have something to tell you about your grandfather's death, but until then, Agent Knox? Be careful."

I shiver as the line goes dead, goosebumps rising across my skin. It's what I suspected, and yet, discovering I was correct is no less surprising. And the implication if it holds true after both Butch and Grace's bodies are autopsied no less disturbing.

Because it means there has to be some kind of connection between them. The killer crossed genders, decades of age, and given Grace's surname, one common among those of Seminole ancestry, races.

Which means there's either a very specific reason why they wanted them both dead—or we're dealing with an indiscriminate murderer, someone who takes lives when the mood strikes and because they can, which is the hardest kind of perpetrator to catch.

I refuse to believe that. I can't.

Finding connections is what I do. Just because a computer algorithm hasn't spit out the first step, that doesn't mean I'm at a loss as to where to begin. When in doubt, start with the basics, the facts closest to the victims, before broadening your search. I need to think of how best to do this.

Grabbing my keys, I step outside. Squinting against the sun and the heat and the gnats swarming the air around me, I lock the door, then stride across the yard. Stopping by the barn, I pull on a disposable glove and grab a chicken carcass from the refrigerator. Then I head toward Chomp's pond out back.

I find the alligator sunning himself on the far shore when I get there. I keep an eye on him as I walk around the exterior of the wire fence. He keeps an eye on me, too. Or, more likely, the dead bird in my hand.

As I reach his side of the pond, he takes a step closer to the barrier. Most alligators are skittish. Even large ones will typically jump into the water when a human gets too close. But Chomp isn't most gators. He's habituated.

He was small when he arrived, not quite three feet. He didn't pose much of a threat, and even if he did, he was terrified of humans. Whoever had caused his injury, it was an act he wasn't likely to forget.

Had he remained in the wild, chances are he wouldn't have survived long. Unable to defend himself, he likely would have fallen prey to one of the two predators that alligators face—man, and bigger alligators.

But he did survive. Over the last three decades, he's overcome his fear of people as he's come to associate them with food. And though there's a fence around his pond, that wouldn't stop him for a second.

Even back when he was little, he could have easily climbed to freedom. Now, at over thirteen feet long, he could bulldoze right through it. It was only there in the first place as a safety precaution Butch enacted when I was little. It remained there, and has been patched and maintained over the years, to discourage other creatures from entering Chomp's territory.

I imagine he only stayed because Butch worked so hard to create a nice life for the gator, keeping the pond stocked with fish and throwing in a nice chicken dinner once a week. The alligator's eyes track my movements now as I wind up, swinging that free meal he's looking forward to behind me before tossing it over the fence.

It lands at the edge of the pond with a small splash. Chomp jumps in after it with a bigger one. I turn away as he eats, grab the disposable glove I'm wearing by the wrist, turning it inside out as I take it off and shove it in my pocket.

This back part of the property has been left natural, a thick layer of scrub and brush ceding to dense Florida woods. It's what separates Butch's land from the neighborhood beyond. When I was younger, I used to play back here, forging trails and building forts with my friends.

Sometimes we'd hear other kids playing and would creep through the wilderness until we found them, spying on them through the fence. I wonder if Grace had been one of those kids. What she looked like. What her life had been like before it was taken away.

Pulling out my phone, I google her name. Scroll through the results, clicking on the third one down, curious about the hit, a link for a shop called Native Flair. A moment later, I find myself looking at picture after picture of bracelets, pendants, headbands and belts, purses and wallets, hanging tapestries, even walking sticks and canes adorned with intricate beadwork in traditional Seminole Indian designs.

I toggle to the about page where a headshot of the artist, a woman about my own age, every bit as beautiful as her creations, looks back at me, her dark eyes shining like she knows a secret. And maybe she did. Maybe what she knew got her killed. Because the woman looking back at me, according to the tiny caption under the photograph, is Grace Billie.

My throat tightens as I stare at her picture,

wondering what she might have had in common with Butch—besides Jake. Is it possible that it was his truck outside her house the night she was murdered? I can't reconcile the sweet boy I knew and what I've come to know about the man he is now with being a killer, but maybe I'm wrong. It wouldn't be the first time.

I need to talk to someone who was close to her, her friends, her family, and see what they think happened. Scrolling to the bottom of the page, I highlight the address, click over to the navigation feature on my phone, and paste it into the search bar. Turn back to the house as I hit enter. Spin back around as the directions appear.

Grace must have run the shop herself, out of her home. And it's close. So close, that my phone says it's only a five-minute walk.

I squint into the woods, trying to remember how far in the back fence line is. Wondering if any of those trails my friends and I used to make still exist as I take a step closer to the trees. Knowing that it doesn't matter if they don't. If not, I'll just have to forge my own way. Because I'm going in.

CHAPTER 22

Palmettos saw at my legs as I battle through the woods. Mosquitoes swarm in a cloud around my body so thick that I have to breathe through my barely open mouth to avoid inhaling them. Something slithers away through the brush, drawing me up short.

There's no need to debate the wiseness of my decision. I know what I'm doing is stupid. Stupid and reckless, and possibly deadly.

What if I step on a poisonous snake and get struck? Flush out one of the rare panthers that call the Everglades their home? Stumble into the backyard of an armed homeowner, their trigger finger on edge after the murder of a neighbor?

And yet, I keep going, each step bringing me closer to the little blue dot on my screen. To Grace Billie's house. Because I have to see for myself. I won't be able to do or think of anything else until I confirm that her property directly backs Butch's. This could be the connection I'm looking for.

I forge onward, the way growing more treacherous as the trees get closer together, the brush denser. A tangle of vines spreads through the overgrowth like an infection. Though I try to watch my step, I trip as my foot gets snagged.

Stumbling forward, my arms spin through the air

as I try to catch my balance. Losing the battle, I fall to my hands and knees mere inches from the sharp barbs of a cluster of Devil's Tongue, one of the types of prickly pear cacti native to the area.

Cursing, I carefully work my way into a sitting position and take stock of my injuries as I catch my breath. My neck aches from the snap of the unexpected tumble. My knees are dirt-stained and tender, my palms scraped. But it could have been a lot worse.

A sea of cacti spreads before me, guarding the way with three-inch spines. This is the end of the road, as far as I can go. I curse again, tears of frustration filling my eyes.

Navigation apps are notoriously off, especially in rural areas like this. I need to see with my own eyes, to make sure that what mine shows is true—that Grace lived directly behind Butch. Confirming that their properties were adjacent doesn't prove anything, but it's a start, one that I desperately need.

I cast a forlorn glance in the direction I wish I could go. Squint past the impenetrable fortress of cacti to where they appear to end, at a chest high barrier of green. Beyond it is a flash of yellow.

It takes me a moment to make sense of what I'm seeing—the fence that marks the property line, hidden beneath a jumble of the same vines that tripped me. And just past it, visible only through patches between the dense greenery, is a strip of yellow crime scene tape flapping in the breeze.

Scrambling to my feet, I stand on tiptoe, taking in every detail that I can. A house painted the color of salmon. A brown shingled roof. Far to the left, just barely visible, another building, painted grey. It's not a lot, but it just might be enough.

I retreat, heading back in the direction I came

from as fast as I can, ignoring the ache in my knees. Break into a jog as I spill from the woods, skirting around the pond where Chomp is once again basking on the bank, racing back toward the front of the property.

Bypassing the house, I head straight for my car, jump in, and crank the engine. Travel up the driveway, wrestle the gate open, then drive through, pulling out onto the main road.

It takes mere minutes to reach the branch off to the Sugarcane District. I make the turn, forcing myself to lower my speed as a neighborhood appears ahead. Though the streets split and loop, I keep to the left, to the properties that back up to Butch's.

A home the color of salmon with a brown roof appears up ahead, and just past it, another home, painted grey. This is it. This is what I saw.

I pull to a stop, park along the curb, and exit the vehicle. Stand staring at the house, at the yellow crime scene tape strung across the front door, for a long moment before searching the street around me. There's not a person in sight. So I start walking.

Passing Grace's place, I head for the grey house next door, but the driveway's empty. A For Sale sign in the yard bears a placard that boasts SOLD. As does the next house. And the next.

Where are the neighbors? The ones who supposedly saw Jake's truck parked outside Grace's house the night she was killed?

A shiver of apprehension ripples through me. The street has an eerie feel to it, like a place long abandoned. Most of the houses appear vacant.

I peer at the empty driveways that stretch ahead of me, then turn a slow one-eighty, searching for signs of life. My palm caresses my hip, but there's no firearm strapped to my side.

The hair on the back of my neck bristles. My heart gives an irregular beat as I change direction, hurrying toward where several vehicles are parked past my own, lips parting with a sigh of relief as a door opens ahead.

Voices carry through the humid air. One of them is familiar.

Ducking behind my car, I watch through the window as Gordon and a couple approach the street. They talk briefly on the sidewalk, then separate, waving goodbye as Gordon climbs into his truck, the couple into a maroon sedan.

I stay where I am, hidden, until both vehicles have disappeared. Until I'm alone again. Just me and my growing sense of uneasiness.

CHAPTER 23

My hands shake as I duck inside my car, locking the door behind me. I pull the seat belt across my chest, latch the buckle, and then I… just sit there, staring into the rearview mirror, watching the now empty spot where Gordon had been with the couple, replaying what I'd seen over and over again as I try desperately to make some sense of it.

Finally, once the heat builds inside the closed vehicle, I'm forced to turn the engine on. Putting the car in gear, I drive ahead, exploring the rest of the neighborhood in front of me. Even the houses without sale signs appear empty. Porches without flowerpots, yards without grills or toys, there's not a personal touch anywhere, nothing to suggest that anyone will return to cook dinner, or watch TV, or tuck their kids in to sleep later tonight.

Just empty window after empty window, each a blank slate. But where are the new owners? Even if the houses have sold, surely someone would be moving in.

Unless… reaching the cul-de-sac at the end, I change direction, remembering how Gordon had said he had a developer friend who would kill for Butch's property. I'm beginning to wonder if he meant that literally.

Rolling my window down, I come to a stop in

front of one of the sold properties so I can take a picture of the sign and look up the transaction when I get home. The image snags as if drawn sideways by an invisible finger as I snap the shot, an incoming call causing the glitch.

Immediately, I think of the medicolegal investigator's promise that the detective working the case would contact me once Butch's autopsy had been completed. I answer without a second thought, not realizing it's a mistake until a familiar voice makes my lips curl in distaste.

"Agent Knox."

"Dr. Parsons."

"I won't take much of your time. I'm just calling to follow up on our last conversation, to make sure that you've made an appointment with the psychiatrist I suggested."

I swallow hard, struggling to think of something I can say that will get me out of this, but I'm pulling a blank. Sometimes you just have to take accountability and face the heat.

"No, I'm sorry, I haven't yet."

Silence. I check the phone, but the timer is still active, the call hasn't dropped. Finally, he says, "I see," his voice grave with disappointment.

"There's been a lot going on here. I've had my hands full."

"Your grandfather's funeral was Saturday, correct?"

"Well, it was supposed to be."

"What does that mean?"

I clear my throat, trying to decide how much to reveal. "There's been a... complication. Some bruising that suggests his cause of death might have been incorrect. They've decided to perform an autopsy."

His voice is softer as he says, "I'm sorry to hear that."

"I admit, it's been a bit of a shock. Especially considering another body has been found, murdered the same way. The woman lived—"

"Did you say murdered?"

"I… Yes."

"And what does this have to do with you?"

Reaching the stop sign at the end of the street, I stay there, engine idling.

"The woman, she lived right behind my grandfather's property. And there's something really weird going on. Her whole street is vacant. I'm here now and—"

"Agent Knox."

"Some of the homes appear to have sold, but the really concerning thing is that I saw someone I know come out of one of the houses."

"Agent Knox."

"I went to school with the guy, we used to be friends, and what makes it so strange is that he told me he had a developer friend who would *kill* for my grandfather's property and—"

"Agent Knox!"

I fall silent, my ear ringing.

"Are you listening?" he asks.

"Yes."

"Good. I want you to seek treatment immediately."

"For what?"

"It's my opinion that you're experiencing a psychotic episode of some kind. What you're describing are most likely paranoid delusions."

"You think I'm imagining all this?"

"I do."

My heart spasms in my chest as I consider the possibility. Could I really have concocted everything I think is going on?

No. If he wants me to admit that I've had a panic attack or two, fine, but I'm not losing my mind.

"You're wrong."

"Excuse me?"

I can understand why he's surprised. He never knew the old me, just the broken version who sat in his office meekly nodding her head at whatever he said. But that spine I seemed to have lost has grown back.

"I said, you're wrong. If you don't believe me, call the Collier County Medical Examiner's Office and ask. Otherwise—you know what—no. Either way, get off my back. You're not helping."

"I'm afraid I'm going to have to let Director Jacobson know about what you're experiencing."

"Don't bother. I'll save you the trouble and tell her myself right now."

Hanging up, I stare at the phone, panting, for only a moment before dialing my superior officer's number. Reaching her voicemail, I leave her a message, still breathless as I tell her that Dr. Parsons thinks that I'm delusional because I stood up to him, but that I'm fine.

That there's no need to call me back, I just want her to know that the shrink reacted poorly to meeting the real me. Then I toss my cell onto the passenger seat and continue the drive home.

I may have just set what was left of my career on fire, but if I'm going down, I'm going to make it a blaze of glory. I'm done being told what to do. Tired of questioning every decision.

Worst case scenario, Butch gets his wish, and I stay here. Best case… well, once I figure out what it is that *I* want, I suppose I'll know what that is. Until then,

I have a murderer to catch.

Exiting the neighborhood, I wait for a truck hauling a horse trailer to pass before turning onto the main road. I'm making a mental list of everything I need to do when the flash of brake lights ahead draws my attention. Instinctively, I slow.

The pit of my stomach fills with dread as I watch the trailer pull into the next driveway. The sanctuary's driveway. I need only one guess as to what they're trying to do. And I was in such a rush earlier that I forgot to close the gate, leaving them the perfect opportunity to do it.

I pull over onto the side of the road. Fight against the fingers of panic trying to curl themselves around me. Tell myself that there's nothing to be afraid of. I'm the one who made it out of that basement. Only me. Yet my body still tries to betray me by succumbing to fear.

The rational part of my brain knows that what I'm experiencing is a set of physiological responses that I can't control, so I focus on the things that I *do* have power over. Getting out of my car, I take deep, even breaths, paying close attention to the feel of the ground beneath my feet as I walk toward the driveway, my gaze pinned to mailbox.

I can do this.

When I reach the mailbox, I turn into the driveway. Briefly debate locking the gate Jake rigged, trapping the would-be zebra-nappers inside, before I rule it out. The last thing I need is to face charges for false imprisonment. So I leave it open behind me as I walk through, my eyes fixed to the barn in the distance.

With each step, I feel a bit calmer. My thoughts slow. My muscles relax.

I long to run into the house and find Butch's gun, but that would only escalate the situation. Besides, I don't think there's time. Whoever was in the vehicle is already in the barn. Their plan is already in motion.

My pace quickens, realizing I need to reach the barn before they emerge. With any luck, the wire rope clip I put on Daisy's stall is slowing them down. With a lot of luck, they're too stupid to figure out how it works.

Passing the truck, I peer through the window, hoping the driver left the keys inside. Decide I hate push button ignitions as I continue on, so close now that I can hear raised voices arguing inside.

"I can't get the dang thing open. You try again."

"There's no time. You'll have to climb inside. You can pass the baby to me. One zebra is better than no zebra."

I grab the pitchfork from where I left it that morning, propped against the empty wheelbarrow just outside the door. Then I step inside.

"I'm not going in there. What if the momma zebra attacks me?"

"What if she doesn't?"

"What if you leave here with the same number of holes in your body that you came with?" I ask.

Both men turn startled looks in my direction. I don't recognize either of them. Either Jeff Gates, the scum who owns Surfing Safari Animal Experience, sent someone else to do his dirty work, or there are multiple people after Butch's zebras.

"Who are you?" the bigger one asks.

"FBI Special Agent Cassidy Knox. Also known as the property owner. And you're trespassing."

"FBI?"

"Correct."

Adrenaline surges through my veins as they stare at me. I stare back, tension crackling like heat lightning in the space between us.

"I don't care who you are," I say. "Only that you leave now, without the zebras, and never come back. If that doesn't work for you, I'll get out of your way. I'll even give you the chance to get down the road a bit. But you should know that the punishment for horse theft under Florida law is still death by hanging."

One mutters to the other, "Is that true?"

"I assure you, it is. Go ahead and google it. I'll wait," I offer.

The two men exchange a glance. My hands tighten on the shaft of the pitchfork as I walk farther into the barn, so they won't have to pass by me to get out. My chest is growing tighter, my breaths shallow. I try not to think about what will happen if they both decide to come at me at once. If I succumb to the panic trying to take hold.

The bigger one curses. Eyes me as he backs toward the doorway. His companion follows suit.

A moment later, the truck engine roars to life. I close my eyes, listening as the vehicle drives off, before making my shaking legs carry me outside to confirm that they're gone. Then I hike back up the driveway to collect my car knowing that next time, I might not be so lucky.

CHAPTER 24

I'm shaky. It feels like my veins are filled with pure adrenaline as I hurry into the house, heading straight for Butch's room. Opening his closet door, I look inside. Rising up on my toes, I feel blindly until my hand closes around what I'm looking for.

Pulling the metal box from the shelf, I stare at it, knowing the immense responsibility that waits inside as I carry it to my room. Taking a seat on the bed, I cradle it on my lap. Removing the key from the strip of masking tape affixed to the bottom, I insert it in the lock.

There's a soft click as the tumblers retreat. I lift the lid, hesitate for only a second before setting the box beside me and lifting the gun from within. The weapon is older than I am, the metal dull and tarnished. The .357 snubnosed revolver is almost tiny enough to fit in the palm of my hand, but that doesn't make it any less deadly.

I open the cylinder, confirm that it's loaded. Flinch, almost dropping the gun as my phone rings. Setting it back in the box, I close the lid and turn the key. I shouldn't be carrying right now. I'm still too skittish.

And I know it won't solve any of my problems. But there's something comforting about knowing it's here, should I need it. I answer the call as I place the key in my nightstand drawer, then slip the box onto the shelf in my own closet, arranging old stuffed animals around it with my free hand to make sure it's concealed.

"Hello?"

"Agent Knox?"

My fingers tighten into a fist, strangling the worn stuffed tiger I slept with until I was seven.

"Yes."

"My name is Detective Miguel Torres. Rich Bailey from the medical examiner's office gave me your number. I hope you don't mind."

"No, not at all. Of course not."

Forcing myself to release the tiger, I cross back to the bed, sitting before my legs have a chance to fail me as the man continues. "I'm calling to let you know that your grandfather's postmortem has been completed."

"And?" I ask, squeezing my eyes shut.

"I'm sorry," he says. "Your suspicions have been confirmed. Tissue damage consistent with strangulation injuries was discovered."

The seashell sound of the ocean thunders in my ears. There's no joy in being right about something like this. It isn't a victory. Butch deserved the best this world had to offer. Instead, he was murdered.

"I see. Have you spoken with the physician who signed off on his death certificate? The one who attributed his cause of death to a heart attack?"

"I haven't yet, but I plan to."

"Do you believe his case is in any way related to what happened to Grace Billie?"

"Given your profession, I'm sure you understand that I shouldn't be discussing that with you right now."

Dejectedly, I admit, "I do."

"But I'm guessing I can also count on your discretion. So yes. Between you and me, due to the number of similarities between the marks found on his body and Ms. Billie's, it's likely that the same ligature was used. Which means it's probable that the same person is responsible."

"I think it has something to do with their land," I say. "Her property directly backs my grandfather's. And the whole street looks like it's been vacated. Most of the houses appear empty."

"I'll keep you posted on what we find."

His response feels dismissive. My gut is screaming that I'm on to something. But once again, it appears that I'll have to pursue that something by myself.

So I let him end the call without pushing the issue any further. It would be nice to have some help, but perhaps it's for the best. Because if I'm mistaken…

Screw that. There's a chance I'm on the wrong path, sure, but I'm tired of second-guessing myself. That's what gets you in trouble. What tricks you into letting your guard down. I'm not making that mistake again.

If I have to work this angle alone, so be it. I'll do it. Starting now. Grabbing my laptop, I head to the living room, settling on the couch.

The first thing I do is order what I think I'll need to properly secure the barn. It's too hot here to close the doors and windows, especially during the day, but an abundance of surveillance equipment, motion sensors, and floodlights should help deter would-be thieves. And a satellite Wi-Fi connection so nothing can be disabled with the clip of a wire.

Then, I see what Google has to say about Gordon. It seems my old friend has done well for himself as a local real estate agent.

It's likely that he was in the Sugarcane District neighborhood earlier today in a professional capacity, considering that a quick look at his profile shows that he's represented either the buyer or the seller in a number of recent deals there lately—and there've been a lot.

Where's everyone going? Why the mass exodus?

Unable to find any mention of a reason why the neighborhood would need to be vacated online, I bring up the picture I took of the sale sign earlier and call the listing brokerage's number. The call is answered after the first ring by a pleasant woman who sounds too young to have been working long.

"Blue Fin Realty, how may I help you?"

"Hi, I'm calling about a property I'm interested in. Your name was on the sign. I was hoping to arrange a showing."

"That's definitely something we can help you with," she says enthusiastically.

I rattle off the address, listen to the sound of her fingers on the keyboard.

"I'm sorry, ma'am, it appears that house has sold already. Would you like me to transfer you to one of our agents so that they can discuss other listings with you that might meet your needs?"

I would, but I'm afraid that Gordon might be the one to take the call. I don't know if he'd recognize my voice or not, but it seems too risky to chance.

"That's really the neighborhood I'd like to be in. I don't suppose you could tell me if there are any other houses for sale in that area."

There's not a pause, not even the click of a key before she says, "I'm sorry, there's nothing."

Thinking of all the other houses that had signs in the yard, I ask, "Are you sure?"

"Yes." Her voice has gone tight. Suddenly, she doesn't sound so young anymore.

"Well, is there some kind of list I can get on to

get an alert if a new property in the area comes on the market?"

"No."

"Would it be possible to—"

"I'm sorry, ma'am. A customer just came through the door."

I expect her to ask if I mind holding. Instead, she hangs up. I frown at the phone, wondering if the call dropped, because I'm fairly certain that it's not normal for real estate brokerages to turn away customers, but the bars on the screen show full reception. I get that familiar feeling, the one I used to chase after, the one that lets me know that I'm on the right track.

I need to speak with someone involved. Someone who has nothing to gain by being cagey and keeping secrets. I need to speak with one of the sellers.

Using one of the mainstream public real estate websites, I make a list of all the addresses in Grace's neighborhood that have been reported as sold recently. Then I start looking up digital copies of the deeds used to transfer the titles of those properties, making a list of names.

A dozen documents into my search, something familiar catches my eye. It's not one of the bits of information that I've been collecting. In fact, I almost miss it.

Going back for a second look at deeds I've already worked through, I confirm the discovery. And as I check the rest of the properties on my list, I find it's something that they all have in common. Electricity crackles beneath my skin, shooting bolts of lightning through my limbs. This feels like something dangerous.

Because the buyers all have more in common than their new homes on the same street. According to the addresses listed on the deeds, their old homes were all on the same street as well.

Whatever I've just stumbled upon, it's big.

This is more than I should try handling on my own, especially with the resources currently at my disposal. But I'm reluctant to ask Mallory for another favor when I haven't heard from her yet about Myers and Kleinman. She has a job to do, and it doesn't include conducting unsanctioned research for a friend.

But it seems odd that she hasn't contacted me. Has she not found anything? Is she ignoring me? Or is it something worse than that—has she been instructed not to help? Told that I'm having a mental breakdown, that I'm delusional, even?

I glance out the window at the darkening sky, disappointment so thick on my tongue it has a taste, like bile mixed with wood shavings. Because whatever my next move is, it's going to have to wait. Night is falling, bringing with it its own set of risks. And I need to be ready for them.

CHAPTER 25

It's pitch-black. The ground beneath me is cold and hard, dirt judging by the soil now under my fingernails. The air is dank, thick with the scent of mold.

My entire body throbs with the need to move, some muscles bunched into knots, others stretched uncomfortably far. But I stay as I am, curling only my toes inside my shoes, my fingers trapped behind my back, to keep the blood flowing.

Because the handcuffs that bind my wrists are too tight to escape. The metal pole that they're looped around much too thick to be broken.

So I listen. And I wait.

For how long, I couldn't say, only that my palm is bloody from the number of times I've dug my nails into it to stay awake. The chill has wormed its way through my flesh, into my bones. I'm starting to worry that no one's coming. That I'll be stuck here, wherever I am, forever.

And then I hear it.

It's faint at first, the groan of a floorboard somewhere overhead. The slide of a bolt. The creak of hinges. Even the flick of a switch is loud after being alone in the dark and the quiet for so long, the light painfully bright through the thin skin of my eyelids.

It takes all my effort to stay as I am. To remain

still. To keep my eyes shut.

I'm desperate to take a look at my surroundings. At the man whose gaze I feel raking over my skin. But I focus all my effort on waiting. Drawing slow, steady breaths, not even letting my muscles tense.

After what seems an eternity, there's motion again, the air stirring as he moves almost silently, the soles of his shoes mere whispers on the stair treads. The scent of musty dirt tickles my nose as his steps disturb it, bringing him so close that I can hear his breathing now.

The light filtering through my eyelids dims as he blocks the source. Still, I don't move. I don't move. I don't move. Until I do.

I strike out, then curl in on myself, scooting backwards frantically, trying to get to safety. Gasping as I struggle to catch my breath after the explosive movement. As I prepare for my next attack.

"It's okay."

Though I register the differences—the warmth, the familiar odors, the miniature goat staring at me warily—I can't process them quickly enough. I only know that I have to get away. That even when I do, this is not something that ends well.

"Ssh, Cassie, it's okay."

Strong arms wrap around me. I snap forward, trying to escape, but they hold tight. I'm trembling so hard that it's a miracle they aren't shaken free. Panting so loud it's amazing that I can still hear the gentle voice, now whispering in my ear. The jeaned legs on either side of me end in a pair of worn work boots, blurry through the tears spilling from my eyes to trail down my cheeks.

I press myself farther into the embrace, grasp at the arms around me with hands that barely work, silently begging him not to let go. And they don't. Not as my breath comes back to me or my tears stop or as my muscles twitch, relaxing by degrees.

It's been silent for what seems like a very long time when Jake asks, "Are you all right?"

I nod, my voice cracking as I say, "Just a bad dream."

"That must have been some nightmare." When I don't respond, he asks, "Want to tell me about it?"

"No."

"Are you sure? Sometimes it helps to let it out."

I watch as Stephano approaches timidly, feeling horrible that I scared him. He sniffs, scenting for danger. Knocks his head against Jake's leg, *baas*, then retreats to the old horse blankets piled on the ground that he's claimed for his own.

"Does the nightmare have anything to do with that panic attack you had the other day?"

At the mention, I feel my muscles draw tight, my chest constrict. Jake's hand strokes my head, impossibly gentle and soothing.

"You can trust me, Cassie. You know that."

I start talking before I have a chance to think about the decision, because I need someone to trust. Desperately.

"I'm not a field agent," I admit. "I spent my entire career in a tiny room at the Bureau, analyzing data, until last year."

I fix my gaze on the goat, now curled into a ball on the blankets. Watch the even rise and fall of his body as he drifts back to sleep.

"I worked so hard to get out of that room. To not just identify cases, but to work them. I wanted to solve crimes. To bring killers to justice. And finally, I was given the opportunity to show them what I could do. Not on active cases, just cold ones, but that was good enough for me."

I focus on the feel of his arms around me. Of the safety they promise, knowing full well that it's just an illusion.

"I even got a partner, though he hated me," I smile as I say it, though my heart feels like it's being wrung out like a wet dish towel.

"So I did everything in my power to prove my worth. I spent hours poring over the files for the job we were assigned, analyzing even the smallest detail. I contacted the agents who originally worked the case, the loved ones of the victims, everything. Until finally, I found it. The thing that everyone else had missed."

I tuck a lock of hair behind my ear, several strands tugging free from where they've stuck to the salty tears now dried on my cheek.

"My partner thought I was chasing my tail, especially when I found a link between my suspect and another case. Another series of cases, actually, active ones. He didn't think the killer would change his MO so drastically, and I admit, it's rare, but it happens, and in this case, it had to, because it would have been too obvious if two of his students fell prey to the same serial killer."

The beat of Jake's heart against my back quickens.

"Since my partner didn't believe me, I went to go speak with him myself, just to feel him out. He seemed so nice at first. So normal that he had me doubting myself. But the moment I showed my credentials… They found the canister in the house, later. Halothane. A small cylinder of it that he kept mounted to the wall next to the front door, like a fire extinguisher. I was unconscious before I even realized what was happening."

He's breathing hard now, but he doesn't interrupt, doesn't stop me even though I know he doesn't want to hear any more. I don't want to say any more. But I have to.

"I woke up in total darkness. It didn't take me long to figure out I was in a basement, handcuffed to a metal support beam. There was no escape. I knew there was only one way I was getting out of there alive. So I pretended to be unconscious. Stayed in the same position I woke up in for I don't know how long, until he came to check on me. Until he got close enough. Then I kicked out, knocked him off his feet."

I tell myself it's just a story. A cautionary tale, or something that happened to someone else. That the scars that resulted aren't mine to bear, even if they've been branded into my skin—some of them quite literally.

"He hit his head when he fell. While he was stunned, I kept kicking him, driving my heel into his throat until… until I knew I was safe. Then I pulled him close enough to me with my feet that I could spin around and use my hands. The cuff key was in his pocket."

"Cassie."

But I'm not done, I was only taking a breath.

"I didn't know that I had been missing for two days. That my partner had come looking for me. I was just sitting there, free. Catching my breath. I was sitting there, when I should have been on the move, should have left already, when all of a sudden, I hear a gun fire. I got to my feet, ran up the stairs, but I was too late. The man—Harold Griggs—had his house booby trapped. My partner had tripped one of the wires."

My voice falters, the lump in my throat impossibly big. I have to choke out the worst part of what happened that day.

"He took a close-range shotgun blast to the chest. He was trying to help me. If only I had gotten up, escaped instead of sitting in that basement like an idiot. If only I had done what *anyone* else would have…"

I wipe at the tears in my eyes, amazed that I still have any left. Not telling Jake the real reason I was still in that basement. That I could feel the ooze of the wound on my back, ripped open during my struggle, as I scanned my surroundings for the shirt I hadn't been wearing when I woke.

"Cassie, it's not your fault."

"But it is. His blood is on my hands."

"It isn't. You didn't know he was there, or that the house was rigged. And you'd, I mean, after what you'd just done, of course you'd be out of breath. You can't blame yourself for taking a moment."

"Everyone else does."

"Are you sure about that?"

"Yes. Because if I hadn't waited, my partner would still be alive."

"But you might not be."

"What do you mean?"

"If you had gotten up those stairs before your partner got shot, it might have been you who tripped the wire."

I hadn't thought about it that way before. I've been so busy blaming myself, dealing with the fallout, trying to evade the fear that stalks me and pinpoint the moment when I made such a horrible, deadly mistake, that I haven't had time for much else. Not until I came down here and got sidetracked by a completely different set of problems.

"Maybe it should have been," I say.

"If you believe that, you need to have your head examined."

"It has been. Repeatedly."

He shifts his arms over mine, intertwines our fingers. "I'm glad it wasn't you," he whispers, his breath hot on my neck.

What begins as a shiver ends as a shudder. Because the heat on my neck, on my throat, has reminded me of other things. Things that make me realize how negligently vulnerable I made myself tonight.

"Were you watching me sleep?" I ask.

"Yes."

"Why didn't you wake me?"

"Because you've looked like you haven't been sleeping well lately. I was hoping you'd get as much rest as you could."

"So you watched me?"

"With everything that's been going on around here? You better believe it. The real question is, what were you doing sleeping out here in the barn where anyone could have found you?"

"I was trying to keep the zebras safe. Not that I was doing a very good job of it if I slept through you coming in the barn."

"What are you talking about? What danger are they in?"

"There was a guy from Surfing Safari Animal Experience here the other day who was trying to take them. I made it clear that would never happen, but…"

"What?"

"Today when I got home, there were two men here with a horse trailer. They couldn't figure out the clip I put on the door, so they were talking about climbing into the stall and lifting the baby out. I don't know if they were sent by the first guy, or if it's someone else who wants them, but I wasn't going to give anyone the chance to try again."

Jake curses. "That's it. I'm staying here. I'll set my tent back up."

"And what?" I pull away, sitting forward until I

can turn to face him. "Sleep out here until the baby gets too heavy to lift?"

"If that's what it takes, yes."

I want to tell him he's crazy, but I don't. A large part of me wants him here, where he can help me keep an eye on things. The rest of me thinks it's the stupidest decision I've made since I didn't get up and run out of that basement the instant I was able to.

CHAPTER 26

My head feels heavy, my mind groggy. I never managed to get back to sleep after waking from my nightmare in the barn last night, though I spent hours tossing and turning in my old bed once I came inside.

The darkness just felt too dangerous. The silence too ominous. My demons too close. And now I worry that I may never sleep again.

The image on my laptop screen looks like something from a dystopian horror movie. Though there are signs that man once inhabited the area—cracked, crumbling roads, a stack of abandoned piping, trash caught in the half-dead brambles scattered among the ruins—it has the appearance of having belonged to a long-lost civilization.

There are no houses, or cars, or signs. The earth itself is a sickened wasteland. The only indication that this place exists in modern times, that it's not a picture taken after crash landing on the planet millennia in the future, is the metal rectangle of a community mailbox in perfect condition.

This isn't a scene from a movie—but it might be a harbinger for the future if I don't figure out what's going on here.

What I'm looking at is a real-time satellite image of the addresses used by the new owners of the properties on Grace's street. My stomach twists and knots on itself as I try to reconcile something like this happening to the land in Gator Glade. To the sanctuary.

Whatever's going on, I have to stop it. I just have to figure out what *it* is first.

The muffled thump of a car door slamming carries from outside. My heart drums nervously, eyes darting to the window, but I can't see the vehicle from where I sit. My mouth goes dry, though my throat keeps trying to swallow.

I know I should find out who's here, but something about the timing of this person's arrival—while I'm looking at a satellite feed of the desolation that awaits my hometown—has me debating whether I should go for Butch's gun first, while I still have a chance. Before I can decide, they knock.

Though I tell myself I'm being paranoid, I can't help wondering what kind of reach the people behind the destruction on my laptop screen have. Their pockets are certainly deep enough. Every single property that's been purchased has been paid for with cash.

Granted, property values in Gator Glade aren't what they are in other areas of Florida, but still, we're talking a lot of money. And with that kind of money comes power.

I consider not answering, but my unexpected visitor knocks again, louder, more insistent. And why not? It's not like they don't know I'm here. My car's parked right outside.

Deciding there's no use putting off the inevitable, I decide this is one fear I should face today. Placing my computer in sleep mode, I rise on legs that feel made of overcooked pasta. Dry my damp palms on my shorts as I wobble across the room and open the door.

"Hey." Alicia gives me a huge grin despite not

knowing how happy I am to see her. "Sorry I didn't call first. Is now a good time? I was hoping to see the zebras."

"Now's a great time," I say.

She claps her hands together, her glee evident. She turns to lead the way toward the barn, then spins back to face me before I can take a step.

"Oh, hey. Sorry. I'm being insensitive. Did you, you know?" She gestures toward the kitchen, where Butch's will still sits on the table.

"I did."

"The zebras belong to my new bestie, don't they?" She winks to lighten the mood, to let me know she's kidding.

I nod.

"Have you decided what you're going to do with it all yet?"

"No. I have no idea, to be honest."

"Well, I'm sure you'll figure it out. And if you decide to make a clean break of it, I doubt you'll have any problem offloading this place. Believe it or not, Gator Glade's really become popular in recent years. I have no idea why, but it has."

Don't I know it. It's just too bad she doesn't have any theories to share, though she keeps up a steady chatter as we walk to the barn, catching me up on the local gossip. I don't have the heart to tell her that most of the names she drops sound only vaguely familiar. Not that I mind. It's a welcome reprieve from my paranoia and conspiracy theories.

Stephano runs over as we come to a stop in front of Daisy's stall. I scoop him up to keep him from jumping on Alicia and getting her dirty. She's so wrapped up in the story she's telling me about a scandal concerning one of the local teachers that it's several minutes before she notices where we are. Then suddenly,

"Ooohhhh!"

It's so shrill that I wince. Stephano's ears flick back, pinning until it's over as he struggles to get down. The moment I set his hooves back on the ground, he scampers off.

"She's absolutely precious!" Leaning against the door, she reaches her arm as far as she can, snapping her fingers and calling to the foal, "Baby! Come here, girl. Come see Auntie Alicia."

Neither zebra is impressed. Though Daisy keeps a wary eye on the loud newcomer, the filly ignores her, turning her back as a beetle catches her attention.

"They don't like me," Alicia says, turning toward me with a pout.

"Hold on a sec. Let me get you a carrot."

I leave her by the stall and enter the tack room, heading straight for the refrigerator. When I return a moment later, I find that Alicia's wandered away from the zebras, farther into the barn.

"What's that?" she asks, pointing.

"A tent."

"Well, I know that, but what's it doing here?"

"Jake's going to start sleeping out here again."

She gives me side-eye.

"There was another attempt to steal the zebras," I explain. "He's keeping an eye on them while I find another way to keep them safe."

"Well, as long as that's all it is."

"What do you mean by that?" I ask.

"Just… trust me. He's not worth staying in Gator Glade for."

"I thought you didn't know him?"

She plays with her purse strap, readjusting it on her shoulder as she says, "I don't. But when I found out he'd taken an interest in you, especially when you're out here by yourself and that girl just got murdered, I decided to ask around, see what I could find out."

"And?"

"Trouble with a capital T. And not the good, fun kind."

"Like what? What's he done?"

She looks at me, the haughty expression on her face melting. "Oh, sweetie." Wrapping a hand around my arm, she squeezes. "I'm sorry. I wasn't trying to upset you."

"You haven't."

"And you said there was nothing going on between you."

"There's not."

"Good. Keep it that way." My expression must give away some of what I'm thinking, because she asks, "Listen, we're friends, right?"

"Right," I say, the appropriate response coming out on autopilot.

"Well, I'm just trying to look out for you."

I force a smile, not wanting to upset her. After all, she's the one who's still local. Who has her thumb on the pulse of what's been going on here in the twenty years since I left. That makes her a useful ally to have, and definitely not a bridge I want to burn.

"In that case, what can you tell me about Gordon Massey?"

She snorts. "Don't tell me you're interested in ol' Gordo?"

"No."

"Well, that's a shame. For him, I mean, not you. Is he still drooling over you like he did back in high school?"

"What?"

"Girl, don't tell me you never realized that he was

head over heels in love with you?"

"I—no. That's not true. Is it?"

"You honestly never noticed?"

"We used to be friends, that's all."

"Mmhmm. Then why were you asking about him? Huh?" The look she gives me is teasing, but something about it makes me uncomfortable. I pull at my collar, the material suddenly feeling too tight.

"I'm just worried about him, I guess." It's the truth, just not in the way she probably assumes. "He stopped by to check on me after Butch's funeral, and he was acting kind of weird."

"Weird how?"

"I don't know. Just weird. Maybe I should avoid him. I don't want to give him the wrong idea."

"I mean, he's boring, but *completely* harmless. Trust me. When are you going to see him again?"

"Oh. We didn't actually make any plans. I didn't even give him my number."

There's a pause as she stares at me. It feels incredibly awkward, ridiculously long, and I worry that she can see the truth written on my skin. That she's going to call me out and try to pry the real answers from me. Then she bursts out laughing.

"Honestly? That was probably the best move. You won't be here long and I'm a lot more fun to spend time with, anyway. Any time you get bored and want to hang out, just shoot me a text." She pulls out her phone and waves it at me. Grimaces as she sees the time. "Except now. I have to take off unfortunately, but let's get drinks later this week, okay?"

She doesn't wait for my response before hurrying back to her truck. I step to the side, melting into the shadows as I watch her leave.

I'm not sure if she's right about Jake or not, but

as much as it pains me to admit, I'm fairly certain she's wrong about Gordon. I don't think he's harmless at all. Because sometimes, the wolves wear sheep's clothing.

CHAPTER 27

This town's starting to have the same claustrophobic feel that it did when I was younger. The only difference is back then I knew who my enemies were. Now they could be anyone. Or everyone.

I need to get out of here for a while. In particular, I need to visit the doctor who signed off on Butch's death certificate. It's not that I don't trust Detective Torres to do his job, it's just that I want to see the doctor's reaction with my own eyes when I ask him the uncomfortable questions he deserves to face. If someone paid him to falsify information, it would be my pleasure to make him the link that breaks.

But I don't dare leave the sanctuary unattended, not until the proper safeguards are in place. So instead, I track the package containing the security equipment I ordered. Thanks to the obscene amount I paid to have the order expedited, it's been shipped, but it isn't in the state yet. Hopefully it will be delivered tomorrow.

Still not ready to delve back into the dark underworld of local real estate, I look up Jake's criminal record. Besides the handful of trumped-up charges Sheriff Kingston brought against him when he was younger—disorderly conduct from a snide comment Jake made that Kingston claimed was an attempt to incite violence, a speeding ticket for driving twenty-eight miles an hour in a twenty-five, jaywalking—there's been nothing since the year after I left town.

I try not to read anything into it. There could be dozens of reasons why Kingston decided to leave Jake alone. Or how Jake managed to stay off Kingston's radar. But it leaves me curious about what Alicia heard about Jake being trouble. I regret not asking more while she was here.

Not that the absence of charges means anything. When I look up Gordon's record, I find that there isn't one. On paper, he's squeaky clean. Maybe I'm wrong about him and he doesn't know what's going on behind the sudden rush of sales. It's possible. Heck, if he's anything like he was when we were growing up, it's probable.

Just because I've become suspicious and jaded, it doesn't mean he deserves for me to think the worst about him. I feel a sudden pang of regret—both that my first instinct was to jump to conclusions, and that I can't trust myself enough to know if that's what I'm doing or not.

This is why I so desperately need to talk to someone who doesn't know any of the people involved. Someone I can trust to tell me if I'm making sense, or if my doubts are unfounded.

I try calling my closest friend, but they don't answer. Not that I expected any differently. I imagine it's a normal side effect of being the reason why someone's spouse was killed, even if I'm slowly starting to accept that it wasn't my fault after speaking with Jake last night.

How can a man like him not be good? My FBI agent brain tries to list dozens of ways, but my heart refuses to listen.

Great. I've become *that* girl. The stupid one who overlooks all the warning signs until she ends up a part of some investigative news special.

I know I need to be smarter than this. But it's more than just the way it feels to have his arms wrapped around me that's making it difficult. Something about him makes me feel accepted, like it's okay to be me, in any of the versions of myself I'm currently struggling with.

That isn't something I can easily ignore. Not when everything else I've experienced lately has left me feeling so insecure. Self-doubt isn't something that I'm used to, and somehow, he eases it, silencing the noise in my mind. It makes me wish I could tell him everything that's been going on.

Butch trusted him. And I know that I can depend on him. So why can't I allow myself to let my guard down?

Because he's hiding something.

I have no idea what, but it's there, in that fraction of an instant of hesitation he sometimes takes before he answers, in how he looks away when I catch him watching me. I groan, feeling like I'm going to drive myself crazy if I don't get some of this off my chest soon.

I turn my attention back to my phone. There are only a couple of contacts I have who I know will answer. There's no way I'm calling the shrink, so I dial Director Jacobson instead.

As far as bosses go, I imagine she's one of the better ones to have. I've always viewed her as a friend as much as a superior. The relief I feel when her soft, calm voice answers makes me worry that I have an unhealthy dependence on the woman.

But I don't let that stop me. I launch right in, telling her about the funeral, about the late autopsy, about Butch's murder, and Grace's. About the link between them I think I've stumbled upon, and the connection I'm sure I've found between property being bought in Gator

Glade and a dusty, now desert town in Arkansas called Tortoise Trails. About would-be zebra thieves and a sanctuary that's now mine to run.

When I'm done, I don't feel better, but I do feel lighter.

"Oh, Cassidy," she says. "I'm so sorry you're having to go through all this. Your grandfather, especially. I'd been hoping this time away would be restorative."

"What do you think I should do?"

I hear her draw a deep breath. "Don't do anything. Not yet."

"But—"

"No buts. Have you told anyone else what you've told me about this property thing?"

"I mentioned that I thought there was a connection between the murders and some recent home sales to the detective working the case, but I didn't go into any detail."

"Good. Give me twenty-four hours. Let me see what I can find out first. Until then, keep all this to yourself. Is there anyone down there you can trust?"

"I don't know," I whisper.

"Then don't. That includes the new psychiatrist Dr. Parsons is trying to get you to see."

"He told you about that?"

She sniffs. "What do you think?"

"That he went tattling like a toddler thinking it would get him all the cookies."

"You wouldn't be wrong. Luckily, I got your voicemail first before I spoke with him. I told him to leave you alone for a day or two, but don't worry about him anymore. I'm going to sign off on your therapy. At least for the time being."

That alone made this confessional worth it.

"In the meantime," she continues, "keep a low profile. I mean it. I know that research is your strong suit, but not this time. You're too vulnerable down there by yourself, so don't do anything. Not a thing. Understand?"

"Yes, ma'am."

"But this is your hometown, so don't be so reclusive as to draw suspicion. See some old friends. Have some fun if you feel up to it. Okay?"

"Okay."

"And Cassidy?"

"Yes?"

"I was worried about you for a while there. It's good to have you back, Agent Knox. I'll talk to you soon."

I sit for a long time after the call has ended, thinking about what she said. About how she'd been worried about me *for a while there*, implying that for her, the worry no longer exists. I suppose it's good that at least one of us has had their fears laid to rest. Because the other one of us? She suspects this nightmare is only getting started, and she's quaking.

CHAPTER 28

Don't do anything. It sounds like it would be easy, but it's not. It gives me too much time to think. To feel. To regret. To inspect every decision I've made over the course of my life with a fine-tooth comb, looking for nits. Spoiler alert—it's infested.

The number of things I'd do differently if I could is overwhelming. Though I'm sure I'm not the only one to feel this way, there's no comfort in it. And with nothing but time to dwell on my past mistakes, I knew I needed a distraction.

So last night, when I finally managed to pull myself together after my call with Director Jacobson, I got to work. I might not be able to do anything I wanted, not without disobeying a direct order, but that didn't mean I couldn't stay busy.

I started with the task I was dreading the most, the one I knew would be the hardest—sorting through the belongings in Butch's bedroom. Though it felt like an invasion of privacy, or worse, a betrayal, I knew it had to be done.

I'm not sure if I can give him what he wanted the most. I don't know if I can stay here, in this house, in this town, but whatever I decide, the space needs to be emptied. Butch wouldn't want a shrine.

He didn't like things to go to waste. As much as

the thought of some stranger wearing something of Butch's pains me, I know that he'd prefer that to the items decomposing in a dresser drawer.

And if I do decide to stick around, I'm going to have to move into his room eventually, no matter how uncomfortable the idea makes me. My childhood room is simply too small, the space almost filled by the twin size bed.

It was only after I was done that I realized a part of me had hoped that I'd find something that would help me make sense of what has happened. What is still happening. That maybe I could make progress on this case without blatantly disregarding the instructions I'd been given by my boss.

But by the end of the night, though his closet was emptied and his drawers cleared, I'd found nothing of interest in that regard. Just a box of mementos with a picture of my parents on top that hurt so badly to look at that I'd hastily put the lid back on and pushed it into the corner to deal with another day.

Only, as I stand in the doorway to Butch's bedroom looking at it now, I realize it's not going to be this day, either. Tossing on work clothes, I pause only to grab an expired granola bar from the pantry and add coffee to my ever-growing grocery list before heading outside. Then I get to work.

By the time the battered UPS truck trundles down the driveway midmorning, I've already fed and watered everyone, walked the fences to inspect them, and swept the cobwebs off the barn walls. I drop everything and hurry over, watching impatiently, eager to get started.

The driver sets down an armful of boxes, shooting me an annoyed look as he returns to the back of the truck for more. I move to join him, my forward momentum stilled by the ping of an incoming text.

Quickly, I pull out my phone, frowning when I see that it's from Alicia.

But my initial disappointment that the message isn't from any of the people I've been anxiously waiting to hear from is quickly overwritten by a smile when I see the GIF she sent of someone in a zebra suit dancing. By the time I've responded, the driver is back behind the wheel, a dozen packages waiting for me in the dirt as he disappears up the driveway.

I spend the rest of the day installing camera equipment, lights, motion sensors, and alarms. Trying to understand instructions written by Martians, intended for rocket scientists. Running wires, driving screws, testing, retesting, and adjusting until I'm such a sloppy mess, covered in a thick coat of sweat and grime, that I have to go inside to take a shower.

The sun has dropped low in the sky when I reemerge, clean and exhausted. I pause, taking a moment to appreciate my surroundings. The freshness of the air. The way the fading light filters through the clouds. Stephano dancing a jig to a tune only he hears.

Say what you will about the heat and the humidity. The insects. The people. I've traveled around the country, visited spots with beauty that left me breathless, but this place right here has something that no other place has. My heart.

My throat tightens with the epiphany, my jaw so tense it aches. I blink against the tears threatening to invade my eyes. Smile sadly as Hildegard, the cow, lows for her dinner. Swallow against the balloon of emotion swelling inside me, the grief that I'm realizing this only now, when it's too late to share it with someone I loved.

This is why I need to keep busy. To stay distracted. Good thing there's still plenty I need to get done before night falls.

Sighing deeply, I continue on my way to the barn. I'm almost there when I hear a vehicle rumbling down the drive. Glancing over my shoulder, I feel a sense of relief when I see the black truck emerging from between the trees. I never know if Jake will be a comfort or a cause of frustration, but either is a welcome distraction right now.

A second later, as I realize that the truck is moving way too fast, that all changes. Spinning, I watch in horror as the vehicle barrels down the drive, where Stephano is amusing himself, oblivious to the danger coming toward him. Breaking into a run, I reach the tiny goat before disaster does, snatching him up in my arms.

Turning my back, I squeeze my eyes shut and brace myself. Instead of a big impact, there are dozens of tiny ones, small rocks pelting me as the vehicle comes to a sudden stop. Rage simmers as, bruised and on the verge of a heart attack, I march toward the barn, trying to escape the haze of airborne dirt that's engulfed me.

A door slams shut. Someone coughs. I find myself hoping that they choke to death so I'm saved the effort of throttling whoever it is. Setting Stephano down inside a stall, I bolt the door, hoping he'll stay inside as I spin to face the intruder. Feel my fury boil over when I see who it is.

"What do you think you were doing, driving in here so fast?"

"Calm down."

"Don't you *dare* tell me to calm down."

"Cass, listen—"

"No. You need to leave."

"We need to talk."

"I have nothing to say to you, Matt."

I find myself looking at the pitchfork I left leaning against the fence earlier. I imagine picking it up.

Using it. Sinking it deep into the meat of his thigh. And honestly? I'm not hating the idea.

It's growing on me. Fast. In fact, if I'm being honest, I'm kind of looking forward to it.

"Go," I say, pointing back the way he'd come so there's no confusion, trying to buy us both a reprieve.

His face screws up in contempt until he's giving me the same look his father's given me many times. "Yeah, I don't think so."

"Well, I do."

I freeze at first, the voice behind me so unexpected that my lungs seize. My body wavers on the edge of panic. But as Jake comes to stand beside me, the fear dissipates. I glance at him from the corners of my eyes to find him glaring at Matt, arms crossed over his broad chest, the sleeves of his T-shirt stretched by muscle.

"What's he doing here?" Matt asks. "Cass, are you sleeping with this guy? You are, aren't you?"

I sigh and roll my eyes. "Go away, Matt."

"Well? Are you, or aren't you?"

"That's none of your business."

"I've heard rumors, but I didn't think there'd be any way you could have turned into that big of a slu—"

Jake launches forward. I throw myself in front of him, hands on his chest, leaning against him with all my weight to keep him from doing something Sheriff Kingston will make him regret.

The brawn under my palms was forged by hard labor, and Matt? He probably hasn't lifted anything more strenuous than a beer can since high school. If this turns physical, the sheriff's son is going to be annihilated.

As much as I'd like to see that happen, had imagined doing it myself only moments ago, I can't let Jake get involved like this. It would essentially be handing him over to Kingston on a platter.

"I guess it's true what they say about swamp scum sticking together," Matt says.

Jake's muscles tense beneath my palms. His breathing is loud, heavy, reminding me of an angry bull. I need to defuse this situation before it becomes a disaster.

"He isn't worth it," I say, loud enough for them both to hear. "Just ignore him. Nothing he says matters. Let's just go inside. Okay?"

Jake looks at me. I give him a small smile. A hopeful one. After a long moment, his scowl eases, and he nods.

"Hey, Walker? I'm gonna grab dinner at Mr. Pizza's later. You know, in case you want some more of my leftovers."

Jake lunges toward him.

"Jake, no!" My hand, not fully dropped from his chest yet, catches him by the waistband on the front of his jeans, a move that makes us both stop short. I swallow hard as our eyes meet. Whisper, "He's just trying to bait you into doing something that will let him get his dad involved. Please don't."

Thanks to Matt, to the lesson I learned early and hard, I've always been on the shy side when it comes to men. Timid. Which is why, when I give the front of Jake's jeans a tug, pulling him closer to me, to the house, my cheeks blaze like they've been set on fire.

"Please," I say again, not entirely sure what it is that I'm asking this time.

The dangerous expression on his face vanishes, his features softening. I take a step backward. He matches the movement, taking one forward. My smile is fueled by more than relief as I continue toward the house with him following. Even as I turn and we fall into step side-by-side, our eyes are still locked.

"I'll save you my crusts," Matt yells after us.

"Trust me," I call back over my shoulder, "he's getting plenty that you've never had before."

"I am?" Jake asks softly, eyebrows arched.

"Mmhmm. Starting with my respect," I tell him.

Though we both hear the names Matt's calling me as he climbs into his truck, neither of us slow down. And as we head inside, I think, *I'm just following orders. Catching up with an old friend like I was told to do.*

CHAPTER 29

Jake and I stand just inside the doorway, staring at each other awkwardly. I have no idea what to say or do next. And neither, it appears, does he. It feels like there's an invisible line drawn between us, one that we're both afraid to cross, because if we take that step, there will be no going back. But if we don't, we'll never know what could be.

"I probably shouldn't have goaded Matt like that," I say nervously.

"I'm glad you did. He deserved it."

"But it's just going to make him more determined to cause trouble. For both of us. He's probably on his way to whine to his daddy right now."

Jake's look darkens, falling into a frown.

"What'd you ever see in that guy, anyway?"

I shrug. "I was fifteen when we first got together. What did I know? He was cute. And popular. I liked how people didn't call me swamp scum when I was with him." My eyes drop to the floor as I add, "And it was different, in the beginning. Good, even. Until he decided he wanted to own me."

Jake curses under his breath. "I should have been there. Done something. I suspected. When I looked at you back then, even when you were smiling, I thought you looked sad. But I told myself I was just seeing what

I wanted to."

"You were there this time."

"Yeah, but you don't need me to save you now."

I didn't need him to save me then, either, though I don't say it. The truth is, if anyone had tried to help, it would have just complicated things. I handled it. I made a plan. I escaped.

It just took me longer than I would have liked. But that was because I had to make sure things ended in a way that would keep the people I cared about safe. The last thing I wanted was Butch getting harassed by the sheriff because of my poor decisions. And in the end, it all worked out.

"You saved me from stabbing him with a pitchfork," I offer. "I was seriously considering it before you showed up. I was kind of looking forward to it, actually."

The storm clouds shadowing his expression lift as he gives me a huge, lopsided grin. "That's my girl."

And like that, the mood shifts. I shift, feeling myself being drawn closer to him as our eyes lock. I swallow hard as he reaches for me, his palms cupping my hips. As the space between us dwindles, I thread my hands under his arms, wrap them around his shoulders, holding on as my head tips back.

His lips lower toward mine. He pauses just before they make contact, his voice low and husky as he says, "You're vibrating."

"I am," I admit.

I really am. Mortification spreads thick beneath my skin as I try to save face, pulling the phone from my pocket. Director Jacobson's name flashes across the screen. Her timing couldn't be worse. I consider letting the call go to voicemail. But this is too important to wait, for any reason.

"Sorry. It's work. I need to take it."

"Yeah, of course." Jake gives me a smile as he releases me, but his disappointment is clear.

"It's my boss. If it were anyone else…"

"You don't have to explain. I still have to finish feeding everyone, anyway."

Guilt strums my chords like a guitar as he turns away, because the animals are my responsibility. But so is this. Duty's calling, so I answer.

"Hello?"

"Are you alone?"

"Almost."

"Let me know when we're good."

A lump forms in my throat as I watch Jake disappear, the door closing softly behind him. A part of me wants to call after him, to tell him to wait. Instead, I sink onto the couch and say, "We're good."

The silence that follows is so long that I'm wondering if she heard me. I'm about to repeat myself, when she finally speaks. "I don't suppose there's any way I can convince you to come home right now? Let us make this someone else's problem?"

My toes go cold inside my shoes, my fingers icy as they curl tighter around the phone. I think about turning my back on the sanctuary. The animals. Their future. On what happened to Butch. There's just no way.

"I can't do that," I say.

Director Jacobson sighs loudly. "I didn't think so, but I had to try. What I'm about to tell you, Agent Knox, needs to stay between you and me, okay?"

"Of course."

"Seriously, Cassidy. This situation, what you've stumbled upon? It's more dangerous than either of us anticipated. You need to be careful."

"I am," I assure her.

"Good. Because this thing goes deep. I've devoted all of my attention to this and I've barely even scraped the surface. We're talking layers upon layers of misdirection, shell corporations, fall guys, and coverups. I'm still working on trying to get more information, but it could take a while, if at all. Until then, there's no telling who's involved."

I crane my head, peering out the window, watching as the hues of dusk gather and bunch to create shadows. As I listen to her, I rub at a spot of gathering tension in my chest until my skin feels bruised and raw. And still she talks.

As she tells me what she discovered about Tortoise Trails, the town all the new owners of the property behind Butch's use for their addresses, it becomes clear why I couldn't find out anything on my own. Because technically, it doesn't exist. At least, not under that name. But the small hamlet of Turtle Glen that used to occupy the same spot geographically did.

Director Jacobson hasn't yet discovered the reason behind why the town was bought and eradicated, but she's found traces—cached pages of blog posts and citizen reports long removed from the internet—that describe how it was done. Not just to Turtle Glen, either, but to almost a dozen different locations, thriving hamlets and neighborhoods that were destroyed seemingly overnight.

In each case, key locals were involved in the downfall. Mayors, trusted community leaders, renowned businesspeople, real estate agents, like Gordon, who begged, tricked, stole, and obviously, in Butch and Grace's case, killed the rightful property owners to gain possession of the land.

Several of the people who posted about what happened had turned up dead, and though the finding in each case was that the deaths were accidental, the more Director Jacobson tells me, the less the likelihood of that being true seems.

By the time the call is over, it's late. Night hasn't just fallen; it's swallowed the earth beyond the reach of the light that filters through the window. I let the curtain fall back into place. Pull up the app for the surveillance equipment I installed earlier to check the feeds, knowing it's something I need to get into the habit of doing before going outside, especially in the dark.

I scroll through the images, feeling relieved when I see Jake's truck still parked behind the barn. I click through the rest of the cameras quickly, check my reflection in the bathroom mirror, then slip through the door, locking it behind me.

Frogs sing from unseen places, their voices rising and falling as one. Grass crunches loudly beneath my shoes. Dew catches the moonlight, making the ground mirror the starry sky above.

A lone light has been left on inside the barn, the low-wattage bulb barely breaking the darkness, casting long shadows. Behind their stall doors, animals stir at my approach. I look at the tent at the far end of the aisle, willing some kind of movement from within. I take hesitant steps closer, until I can hear the low, steady breaths of Jake's slumber coming from inside.

Though I know I shouldn't, I feel the sting of disappointment as I retreat, making my way back to the house. It's past midnight. He has to work in the morning. Of course he's asleep.

But as I let myself back in the house, I wish I weren't alone—not because I seem to have found my way into the middle of some kind of deadly conspiracy, but because I miss having someone to share my life with. It's been a long time since I've felt that way. Years. I thought I was just a solitary person, but maybe… maybe I just haven't found the right company.

And though my first impulse is to run away from the mere idea of allowing myself to be vulnerable, my gut tells me that it would be worth sticking around. That I should face my fears and give this thing between me and Jake, whatever it is, a chance.

Ducking into the kitchen for a snack, my eyes land on the sealed envelope on the table. The one with Butch's contingency plan.

My grandfather was a wise man. When I was growing up, he'd had an almost preternatural ability to predict my behavior. The classes I'd enjoy, the books I'd like, even the ways I'd rebel. At times, I thought he knew me even better than I knew myself.

Had it been a coincidence that Jake's been here all these years, helping him? Or had it been another instance of Butch's uncanny ability to know exactly what I needed?

Lifting the envelope in my hand, I judge its weight. It's light. It can't contain more than a single page. What are the odds that, if I opened it, intent on leaving, it would say only a handful of words? *Reconsider. Think again. You need this, Cassidy.*

Turning on the stove, I work fast, before I can lose my nerve. Touch the edge of the paper to the heat. Watch as the flames slowly crawl up the sides, consuming my excuse to escape. Drop it in the sink as the last little bit becomes ash.

I might need this place, but it needs me too. Someone has to make sure the danger on the prowl is eradicated. And that it stays away. That someone just became me.

CHAPTER 30

When I wake in the morning, the first thing I remember is torching Butch's envelope, the one that contained his instructions for what I should do if I chose not to stay and run the sanctuary. I bolt upright, instantly regretting the decision. Wondering what I could have been thinking.

But I hadn't been thinking, had I? I'd been feeling.

Nostalgia for my hometown. Indignation toward whoever was trying to destroy it. Righteousness over my need to protect it. Rage at the person who has yet to pay for taking my grandfather's life. Lust…

I'm afraid that only one of those things influenced me to stay long-term.

How had I let my libido sway me so strongly? I don't even know Jake anymore. What if the sparks flying between us fizzle out quickly? Or worse, cause an explosion that leaves us both angry and dissatisfied? Now I'll never know Butch's backup plan should I decide I want to leave. How could I have acted so rashly, messed up so badly?

I need to get my hands on another copy of that letter.

Fumbling my phone from the nightstand beside me, I groan when I see the time. It's still early, hours until

Myers and Kleinman will open. In the meantime… opening the app for the surveillance cameras, I check the feeds.

Jake's truck is gone. I watch the videos of him going through the motions of feeding and watering the animals, his image grainy against a dark background. The time stamp as he finally climbs into his vehicle and leaves reads 5:17 a.m.

Given the hour, I can't help but wonder if he was trying to avoid me. Though there's a pain in my chest caused by the thought, maybe it's for the best.

It will give me a chance to work through my emotions. To weigh my options. To make sure I'm not rushing headlong into another mistake. No matter how enjoyable it might be to make.

Shaking my head, I force myself out of bed and into the shower. Dress quickly in the only professional outfit I have with me, the slacks and blouse I wore on the first day of my trip down, then search the house for some paper, finally settling on the small notepad I've been using for my grocery list.

I scroll through the alerts from the security app that have already gathered on my phone, making sure none of them are from detecting a human image. Assured that I'm the only person on the property, I head outside and get in my car.

But my momentum is impeded by the gate blocking the end of the driveway. Jake must have closed it behind him. I stare at it a moment, debating.

Now that I have the security equipment in place, is it really necessary? Obviously, the cameras won't keep someone from taking the zebras, but at least the footage should help me know who to go after to get them back. And if someone's going to snatch them, I'd rather they take them both and keep them together rather than risk injury to either or having them separated.

Finally, I get out and unlock the gate, hauling it out of my way. Once I'm through, I leave it open, trying not to second-guess my decision as I drive away. I can't afford to be distracted. I need to focus.

I have a mounting list of things I need to do today. And all of them involve caffeine.

Ten minutes later, the side road to town appears ahead. I feel a twinge of nostalgia as I remember Beans and Brews, the little café by the water where I had my first mochaccino as a teenager. Their specialty was cinnamon buns the size of your head. I could go for both right now. I wonder if it's still in business.

Unfortunately, today's not the day to find out. I look longingly down the street as I pass by, continuing for another thirty-five minutes until I pull into the parking lot of a bustling chain coffee shop where I feel confident I'll be able to remain anonymous.

The scent when I walk through the door isn't sweet, but bitter, like someone burned the beans before they brewed them. But the place is crowded, no one even glancing in my direction as I get in line, which makes it perfect.

As soon as my drink is in hand, I take a seat at the counter along the window that overlooks the parking lot. Pull out the notebook and a pen, angle myself so no one can see what I'm writing, and stare at the blank page before me. Feel myself frown at the paper, as if it's to blame for my problems, sure this would be easier if I were using my laptop instead.

But that's not an option. Director Jacobson made it clear—no virtual footprints. Actually, her exact orders were to leave this alone completely, but that's not going to happen.

The first thing on my list, the most important

thing, is Butch. If he was killed for his property, which seems safe to assume at this point, it still begs the question: Why?

I mean, obviously because he wasn't going to willingly give it up, but the question goes deeper than that. Why his land? Why Gator Glade? What does this area in South Florida have in common with Turtle Glen, the last place it seems that these people did this to?

Whatever it is, it must be valuable, but all the immediate things that come to mind don't apply. It's not waterfront. This area isn't in high demand, and between the ten months of sweltering heat a year and the size of the mosquitoes—both literally, and their population density—it isn't likely to become so.

Besides, Turtle Glen wasn't redeveloped after it was bought. It was renamed Tortoise Trails and left a barren wasteland.

So, what could it be, then? Natural resources?

In middle school I once wrote a research paper about uranium in Florida. If I remember correctly, one of the largest deposits in North America is in the central part of the state. But that's hundreds of miles from here. Not to mention it seems like something like that would be easy enough to detect. Yet, I can't deny that it's possible. And right now, it's the best I can come up with.

I wrack my brain, attempting to think of other things that could make land more valuable than it appears, but no matter how hard I try, only one thing comes to mind. It's so absurd I'm reluctant to even consider it, but as unlikely as it seems, it's not an option I can dismiss.

Treasure.

I grew up hearing crazy legends about the area. Stories like that of the Lost City, where it was rumored that confederate soldiers buried large amounts of gold stolen from the Union. Al Capone's distillery, where he supposedly hid millions of dollars before he went to jail for tax evasion, money that should have been in his secret vault at the Lexington Hotel but wasn't. Pirates. Yeah, pirates. It's possible.

The Everglades isn't really a swamp. It's actually a slow-moving river system. It's not impossible that a ship sailed this far inland to bury their stolen goods. But if I'm going down such an outlandish avenue as that, there's another to consider.

Because there are some people who believe this area is part of the Bermuda triangle. A number of planes have crashed and disappeared here over the years. Who knows what kind of cargo they had on board?

Or they could be after something that would never even occur to me. Sighing, I jot down who I think would be best to consult about each possibility, then move on to my next big question: Who?

Director Jacobson mentioned last night that locals were typically involved in the takeover. But how many? It's not like there are many people in the area who wield that kind of power. In fact, other than Sheriff Kingston, I can't think of any.

While I wouldn't rule out him being complicit in Butch's murder, he doesn't hold the sway necessary to influence the number of people he'd need to, at least, not without arresting them. And I definitely think something about this would have come to light by now if he'd unlawfully charged that many people.

But what about Gordon? He's well known here. People like him, or at least they used to when I knew him. He's definitely involved somehow—he's been the one selling the properties. And Butch would have remembered him. Invited him inside. Trusted him.

Could my old friend have murdered my

grandfather? Is that something he'd be capable of?

Then there's Myers and Kleinman. They might not be located in Gator Glade, but they're certainly close enough—and powerful enough—to have plenty of influence over the area. I add them to my list, staring at the name.

Why?
- natural resources/geologist
- treasure/historian
- other/unknown
Who?
- Sheriff Kingston
- Gordon
- Myers and Kleinman

I still don't know how they're involved in all this. But I'm about to find out.

I gather my things. Drain the last of my lukewarm coffee, tossing it in the trash on my way through the door. Roll my shoulders back, hold my head high, and prepare to go to battle. I didn't start this war, but I promise myself that I'm going to do my best to be the one to finish it.

CHAPTER 31

The building before me is impressive, six stories of sparkling glass and gleaming metal set atop perfectly manicured grounds, with every shrub neatly shaped, fresh mulch in the garden beds surrounding verdant daylilies in bloom, and not a stray leaf or scrap of trash in sight. A large fountain is the centerpiece of a courtyard with tastefully arranged outdoor lawn furniture, complete with cushions that somehow look spotlessly clean as well as comfortable.

The lobby I step into is no less remarkable. Marble floors, crystal vases overflowing with flowers, real artwork by famous artists on the walls, and a giant chandelier dangling overhead. A desk runs along the far back, the names Myers and Kleinman on the wall behind it.

But I never get the chance at a closer look. The instant I step through the door, I'm greeted by a man armed with a tablet—and a gun. Though the holstered weapon blends seamlessly with the man's black slacks, his posture, crew cut, and mannerisms leave no question—he isn't a doorman. He's security. And the arch over the doorway? It's a cleverly disguised metal detector.

"Good morning, ma'am," he says with a friendly smile. "May I ask who you're here to see today?"

"I'm afraid I'm not quite sure."

His smile hardens. "Do you have an appointment?"

"I don't. I wasn't sure who to make one with."

"Are you a current client?"

"No. My grandfather was, that's why I'm—"

"Then, unfortunately, I'm going to have to ask you to leave."

"What?"

"If you don't have an appointment, you'll have to leave."

"I'll happily make an appointment. That's why I'm here."

He reaches into his pocket, removing a small black box. Flipping it open, he removes a pristine cream-colored business card and offers it to me. "You'll need to make the appointment first."

"Why can't I just make one now?" I ask, pointing toward the desk where two women sit, watching our exchange with bored expressions.

"We take the security of our staff and clients very seriously here, ma'am. No one is allowed in the building without proper verification first."

I flinch as his hand wraps around my arm, turning me back toward the door. Debate the wisdom of shaking it off, not wanting to make any enemies before I've had the chance to speak with someone who might be able to answer my questions.

I glance over my shoulder at the two women as he guides me gently but firmly, the metal detector blipping as he follows me through. One yawns. The other stares at me like I stepped in something gross and tracked it inside. Neither seem to find what's happening odd.

"I look forward to seeing you again once you've made an appointment," the man says as he deposits me on the concrete in front of the building. He offers me the business card again. This time, I take it. "Have a good day."

As he disappears back through the privacy glass door, I find myself wondering exactly what kind of law firm this is. The sparse website had said corporate law, but what exactly do they do here that would necessitate this kind of security?

The answer that comes to mind chills me despite the muggy heat and the anger warming me from the inside out: Take people's homes. Destroy their land. Kill them.

I need to get back in that building.

Retreating to my car, I start the engine, adjust the air vents, then dial the number on the business card the security guard gave me. I'd intended to kill two birds with one stone by coming here today.

I'd hoped to get another copy of the letter that had been included in Butch's will that I destroyed last night, and to find out who it was that he had known here so I could feel out their connection to Gator Glade. Now my goal has changed to include finding out what they're hiding.

"It's a beautiful day here at Myers and Kleinman. How may I direct your call?"

"Yes, I need to speak with whoever was in charge of drawing up my grandfather's will."

"We don't typically handle estates here."

"And yet everything was printed on your letterhead."

There's a long pause, like she thinks if she keeps me waiting long enough, I'll hang up. Finally, she releases an irritated sigh. "What was your grandfather's name?"

"Charles Donovan."

Only several seconds pass before she says, "I'm afraid there's no client in our system by that name."

"Can you try Butch?"

Her tone drips with distaste as she asks, "Butch?"

"Yes. It was a nickname, what his friends called him."

"There's no one by that name, either."

"I don't understand. Someone here drew up a will for him. I need to speak with that person."

"I'm sorry, ma'am. If he wasn't a client, I can't help you."

"But he was a client, that's what I'm telling—"

I look at the phone in my hand, confirming that the call has ended. She hung up on me. How does the place stay in business treating people like this?

Unless it's just a front. Maybe all those offices behind the glass are empty. Or filled with criminals brainstorming ways to take over entire neighborhoods.

But if that's the case, wouldn't Butch's will have told me to sell the property? Instead, it included a letter written in his handwriting telling me he wanted me to stay. It doesn't make sense. None of this does.

My phone rings, the sudden buzzing in my hand startling me so badly that I almost drop it. Hoping it's the receptionist I was just speaking with calling me back, I answer without checking the number.

"Hello?"

"Agent Knox? It's Detective Torres. Is now a good time?"

"Yes," I say eagerly. Maybe this is the universe finally cutting me a break. "Of course."

"I'm calling because, well, I'll be frank. I'm afraid we haven't had much luck gaining traction in this investigation. The avenue we initially pursued has hit a dead end. I know that you requested that we leave the local sheriff out of this if possible, but it isn't. You should know that we've included him in the loop."

I swallow my reply. The last thing I need to do is alienate the man who's supposed to be helping me.

"He said he's been pursuing a lead that came from several of Ms. Billie's neighbors. A local criminal named Jake Walker."

My mouth opens, but I clamp it shut. Director Jacobson told me not to discuss what I'd discovered with anyone. That would include sharing that there's only a handful of neighbors left in Grace's neighborhood. That Sheriff Kingston's 'lead' was most likely false.

Instead, I say, "I know Mr. Walker personally. He's an old friend of the family. He was actually at my grandfather's place with me the night Grace was killed, helping me deliver a foal."

"The sheriff mentioned that. He also mentioned that he thought it was possible that you were a willing accomplice in both murders."

My jaw clenches so hard it pops. "Are you kidding me?"

"I'm afraid not. Any idea why he might suspect you of murder?"

I don't respond with the answer that comes to mind. Instead, keeping my voice calm and steady, I say, "None."

"You requested that he be kept out of the investigation. Why was that?" There's more than just a hint of suspicion in his voice. In fact, this entire conversation is starting to feel more like an interrogation than an update.

I sigh heavily, venting my frustration before responding. "Because I have zero confidence in his ability as a law enforcement officer. He's the last person I'd want responsible for finding my grandfather's killer."

"Sounds like there's some history there."

"Gator Glade is a small town. I dated Sheriff Kingston's son in high school."

"And?"

"That's it. You want details about what kind of a man he is, ask around. I'm sure you'll get an earful."

He grunts in response.

"Well, given that you weren't in the state when your grandfather was murdered, that you're an FBI agent, and that you're the one who brought the suspicious nature of your grandfather's death to our attention, the state police aren't pursuing you as a suspect."

I roll my eyes, grateful that this talk is taking place over the phone. Annoyed that we're even wasting time with this in the first place.

"Were you able to confirm the sheriff's claims that Ms. Billie's neighbors reported a black truck outside of her house the night she was killed?"

"We were."

"Really?"

"Really. Though it does appear that the sheriff may have stretched the truth a bit in his report. There was only one neighbor who saw the vehicle. And he claims to have never mentioned Jake Walker's name, though when I spoke with him, he said he was aware of who your friend is."

"What about the woman's ex-husband?"

"He was piloting a fishing charter that night. I ran his picture by several of the passengers, and they were adamant he was the man out on the water with them. Unfortunately," he says, "that means we're out of suspects. The other day you mentioned something about a connection between your grandfather and Ms. Billie. What was it again?"

I run a hand down my cheek, suddenly grateful he'd been so dismissive when I first mentioned it. "It was just something I was looking into. It didn't pan out."

"You sure? You want to run it by me just in case?"

"That's okay. I'm sure."

"You seemed pretty confident about it the other day," he presses.

If that was his impression, why hadn't he listened? I shift in my seat, suddenly uncomfortable. Check out the windows to see if there's anyone around watching, wondering if the timing of this call is more than just a coincidence.

"I… this is embarrassing," I say slowly, buying myself time to think of a lie. "I haven't been sleeping well, and I thought I found an article online that mentioned them both, but when I went back and looked again, it turned out I had read the names wrong. Both of them. I really didn't want this to be random, but I'm starting to think it just might be."

"Honestly? I'm worried you might be right. But if you think of something, you'll let me know?"

"I will."

After the call ends, I drive out of the parking lot on autopilot, replaying the conversation in my head. What had been the true purpose of the call? Detective Torres hadn't seemed to take Kingston's suggestion about my involvement seriously, so it wasn't that. And he hadn't questioned me about Jake.

Had he really wanted to know about the link I'd found between Butch and Grace? Or had he wanted to know what else I might have discovered while pursuing that connection? Because if that's the case, that means I've made it on the radar of some very dangerous people. Ones who wouldn't hesitate to make me their next target to ensure my silence.

CHAPTER 32

I stare at the building in front of me, debating. I know that I shouldn't be doing this. That I should listen to Director Jacobson and play it safe. But how can I, when the stakes are so high? I have to believe that if she were in my position, she'd be doing the same thing right now.

Which is why I go for it, striding across the lobby of Memorial Hospital with my head held high and shoulders back, passing right by the help desk like I'm confident that I know where I'm going. Which I do. Sort of. At the very least, I know that hospital morgues are usually in the basement. It's just, I don't know if this hospital has one.

The mystery is quickly solved as I step into the elevator, my eyes immediately drawn to the button marked with a B. The problem is, you need to swipe a keycard to access that floor. I push the metal circle anyway, just in case, but it doesn't light up. Which means I'll have to wait for an opportunity to strike.

Twenty minutes later, my stomach complaining from all the trips up and down, a nurse gets on. Leaning past me, she runs the magnetic strip on the ID hanging from the lanyard around her neck and presses the button for a restricted floor. I shift my weight, turning to face her as I discreetly press the B.

"You look familiar," I say, tilting my head like

I'm trying to place her. "Did you go to Glade High?"

"No, Jefferson."

"Oh. Go Dolphins."

She gives me a look that lets me know my small talk isn't appreciated. I step closer to the panel as if giving her space in light of the rejection, though when it's time for her to get off, I give her a concentrated stare.

It has the desired effect of making her keep her eyes averted, so she doesn't notice the circle of light around the button for a floor that she'd know I'm not supposed to have access to. Then I cross my fingers, hoping that my luck holds as the elevator descends.

Moments later the doors open, revealing an empty corridor, the complete silence unnerving compared to the chaotic noise of the other floors. I step off hesitantly, suddenly doubting my decision. But I've already come this far, so I continue my quest, following the signs on the wall pointing the way to my destination.

The first thing I notice when I walk into the room is the air. It's frigid, dry, stale, and carries a slightly fishy odor. The second thing I notice is a man in scrubs wearing a surgical cap and glasses, his arms coated in such a thick pelt of hair that it's hard to imagine that there's skin underneath. Looking up from the paperwork on the desk before him, he frowns.

"You can't be here," he says.

"Actually, I can," I say. It's not technically a lie. The very fact that I'm here proves me right. I flash my badge while I'm still across the room, shutting it before I'm close enough for him to get a good look at it. "I'm Cassidy Knox. I need to ask you a few questions about a body that came in last week, Doctor…?"

"Speck," he supplies with a sigh. "Which body?"

"Charles Donovan."

His look of irritation turns to one of confusion.

"I've already spoken with your partner about that."

"Well, now you're going to speak with me."

I cross my arms and raise my brows, signaling that I'll accept no arguments. He rolls his eyes but gestures for me to proceed.

"Were you the one to complete the death certificate?"

"I was."

"I understand that the initial cause of death was determined to be a heart attack."

"Myocardial infarction," he corrects.

"Myocardial infarction," I repeat with a not so pleasant smile. "Tell me, Doctor. How did you reach that decision?"

He grimaces and removes his glasses. Rubs at the red indentation on the bridge of his nose before replacing them and giving me a look.

"Listen, like I told your partner, it's just me down here."

"And?"

"And as you can imagine, a lot of bodies come through. Many more than the budget supports. The same can be said about the medical examiner's office."

"What does that have to do with the situation?"

He sighs like I'm being purposely difficult. "I'm under a lot of pressure to keep costs down, both here and there."

The doors crash open behind me. I turn to find a paramedic wheeling a gurney into the room. He points to the industrial refrigerator door in the far wall, then gives a thumbs up and continues on his journey.

"Which means that you just wager a guess about what killed someone?" I ask, turning back to the doctor.

"No." He looks contrite as he says, "In this particular case, I went by the information provided to me by the transporter who delivered him."

"Did they tell you why they drew that conclusion?"

I think of Jake's confession about how he was the one who found Butch and realize that a part of me dreads the answer. What if he'd told me only part of the truth? What if I discover that he'd been the one to say that Butch had suffered from a heart attack? I made a conscious decision to trust him. Was that a mistake?

"No," the doctor says. "But if you're curious, you can ask him yourself."

"Who?" I glance over my shoulder at the doors swinging shut. "The paramedic? The one who just left?"

"Yes."

I give him a look that doesn't say a fraction of what I want to tell him. There's no time, not unless I want to risk losing what may be the best lead I've had yet. I jog across the room and out into the hall.

"Hey," I call after the man hurrying away.

My voice echoes in the narrow corridor, causing the paramedic to pause and check who I'm calling to.

"Me?" he asks, pointing to himself.

"Yes. I need to speak with you for a minute."

He watches me curiously, waiting for me to catch up. As soon as I've reached him, he asks, "Do you mind if we walk and talk? I'm kind of in a rush."

"Sure." I fall into step beside him, matching my stride to his.

"What can I help you with?"

"There was a body you transported last week. Charles Donovan. He came from the sanctuary out in Gator Glade."

"I remember."

"Dr. Speck says you told him the man had a heart attack."

"That's true."

"Why?"

"Why what?"

"Why'd you tell him that?"

I watch as he swallows hard. "Am I in some kind of trouble?"

"No. I just need to know what made you come to that conclusion."

My chest becomes painfully tight as Jake's face flashes into my mind.

"I didn't. My partner did."

"Who's your partner?"

"Pat Harvey."

My hearing whooshes like a rocket just flew by us in the hall. But it wasn't an aircraft. It was the ghost of classmates past. Because I know Pat. We went to school together. Were in the same grade. Which makes him very much a Gator Glade local.

Pat and I weren't friends, but that wouldn't have stopped Butch from being friendly toward him, if Pat had stopped by while he was still alive. And Pat would have known who Jake was, which might have made Pat more likely to believe him if Jake was the one to suggest a heart attack.

I suck in a deep breath, trying to find my voice. Finally, I manage to ask, "Did he tell you why he thought that?"

"No. I was talking to the guy who called it in while Pat checked the body." Relief floods my system so hard that I'm shaking with it, almost losing my balance. "I just assumed there were telltale signs. Sometimes there are."

"Like what?"

"Medication vials. Sometimes we find the deceased clutching at their chest. That kind of thing."

"Where's Pat now?"

"I wish I knew."

"What do you mean?"

"He never showed up for work yesterday. I've tried calling and texting a bunch, but he hasn't responded. I'm guessing that means he quit. That's why I'm in such a rush. Not to be rude, but are we done here?"

"Yeah. Thanks."

I stand in the middle of the corridor, watching as he pushes through a set of doors that lead outside. Strategically placed locals—it's just like Director Jacobson said.

Had someone called Pat and instructed him to suggest a cause of death for Butch that would result in an autopsy being bypassed? Had he known all along that it was murder? If so, I can think of another reason why he hasn't shown up for work the last two days. And if it's true, my only regret about it is that he won't have to face my wrath.

CHAPTER 33

It feels like everything's finally starting to make, well, not sense exactly. I still don't know why someone wanted Butch's property so badly that they were willing to kill for it. But the connections are there, I can see that much now.

And maybe that means it's time to back off. Or at least take a break and see what Director Jacobson comes up with. Because I've never been one to gamble. I've always played it safe.

But that didn't exactly do me any good, did it? Not while I was languishing in my career. Or while I toed the line, setting out on my own because I didn't want to upset my partner. And it certainly wouldn't have done me any good in that basement.

So, while there's something to be said about taking the conservative route, maybe that doesn't work for me anymore. Maybe it's time to place a bet, spin the roulette wheel of life, and see if I come up red or dead.

Decision made, I check my surroundings. No other cars have entered the lot since I've been here. No pedestrians have walked by. Assured that I haven't been followed, I get out of my car and walk inside.

The public library has changed since the last time I was here. It still smells like the beguiling mix of old books and freshly baked cookies, but that's the only thing that's familiar.

The small desk where the bespeckled librarian once sat with her too tight bun and her dated rubber stamp is gone, replaced by a long counter staffed by multiple employees. The flickering fluorescent lights that used to hum so loudly they made it sound like you were inside a beehive have been replaced by silent LEDs.

Most importantly, the entire back wall that used to be lined with multiple sets of encyclopedias and a giant card catalog is now home to a long row of computer desks. It's exactly what I'd been hoping for.

I take an indirect route, browsing through shelves of books, now all hardcovers, the dust jackets covered with shiny plastic film, on my way to the far corner. Pulling the latest thriller by a bestselling author free, I pretend to skim the blurb while I check out the workstation beside me.

There's no notice that you have to log your computer time. Nowhere to swipe your library card to begin a session. There's nothing but complete anonymity. It's perfect.

Reshelving the book, I take a seat and bring up the camera app on my phone. I switch it to selfie mode, using it to check behind me. No one's showing any interest in me or what I'm doing.

Still, I take it slow, researching reviews on the book I just looked at. Next, I run a search for rye bread recipes, even though it's my least favorite type of bread. After several minutes, when it still appears that no one's paying attention, I slip the notebook out of my pocket and set it beside the keyboard.

Why?
- natural resources/geologist
- treasure/historian

Reading over the list I'd made earlier in the coffee shop, the only thing that's clear is that my handwriting is atrocious. But that doesn't matter. All that does is finding someone who can help me answer my questions. I need to get to know my opponent, and the only way to do that is to figure out why they're after the sanctuary.

I start with a general search in case something turns up that I haven't thought of: What would make land exceptionally valuable in Gator Glade, Florida?

When that doesn't produce any useful results, I move on to something that I hope will: Who should I talk to about valuable natural resources in South Florida?

This time, the results that populate are more helpful. One in particular catches my eye, the course description for a class at the local university.

Natural Resource Economics of the Everglades. This course provides an in-depth study into the geology, ecology, sustainability, and economy of the Florida Everglades. Students will learn about the supply, demand, and allocation of local natural resources, as well as best practices to preserve and conserve them for future generations.

I click on the faculty page for the professor who teaches the class, writing down his name and contact information, including his office address. Opening a new tab, I look up driving directions, not wanting to use the GPS app on my phone. Read over them a few times until I feel confident that I can get there from memory.

But that isn't the only possible reason I came up

with why someone would want the property, is it? I read my list again, then stare at the screen, wondering if I'm insane. Reminding myself about the whole gambling thing, I type another question into the search bar.

Who should I talk to in order to learn more about treasure in Gator Glade?

This time, I have to wade through two pages of results for obscure Reddit threads, self-professed treasure hunters, and random blogs before I find what I'm looking for.

Local Myths and Legends. This course takes students on a 'deep dive' into the local myths and legends of South Florida. Topics include the Lost City, the "Lost Patrol" of vanished Navy bombers, the origins of the Skunk Ape, the pirate ghost ship of lore, and more. Students will survey and compare both written and oral traditions in an interdisciplinary field that incorporates anthropology, sociology, history, literary studies, psychology, and religion.

Though the logical part of my brain tells me even considering this is an act of desperation, I can't rule anything out. Because I *am* desperate.

I scribble down the professor's name and office number, then clear the browser history on the computer, noticing a great many searches far odder than mine, before I stand to leave. It's time to do a little treasure hunting of my own. But I'm not after gold. It's information I seek.

CHAPTER 34

You'd never know there was anything wrong with the world if you were to judge by the Southwest Florida University campus. Smiling co-eds sit in groups on the grass, gather in the quad, and fill the sidewalks as they walk between classes.

It's a stark contrast to my own college days, most of which were spent in a frazzled state of chaos as I did my best to juggle my class load, coursework, and job. It's also not anything like my present, where my career is in ruins and my personal life is a mess. Maybe one day I'll get to be like these smiling happy people, but if so, today is definitely not it.

I'm sweaty and irritated by the time I find a parking space without a tow warning and hike the mile and a half to campus. I ask three different students for directions, the first two, whether accidentally or on purpose, sending me far from my destination. Finally, I find myself on the doorstep of the Earth Sciences building.

The air conditioning instantly wicks the heat from my skin as I step inside. A shiver quakes through me, my damp clothes making me cold. But as I follow the signs posted on the wall to the office I'm looking for, I find myself chilled for another reason.

First, the claustrophobic stairwell where my

every step echoes off the sickly yellow walls. Then, the empty hallway that appears as if it's been long abandoned. Doors line the corridor, each windowless, concealing whatever's on the other side. Lights flicker overhead as I search the numbered placards for the office I'm seeking.

It feels like a scene from a movie. A lone woman. A deserted building. A jump scare as some sort of villain—a stalker, a zombie, take your pick of monster—springs from the shadows.

I look over my shoulder to see how far I've ventured from the stairwell. Maybe I should turn back. I mean, what are the chances that I'm going to catch the professor in his office? I should have called first. Really, this whole conversation could take place over the phone.

"You look lost."

I flinch, startled, my hand flying to my hip only to find the firearm I'm so used to carrying not there.

"Sorry, I didn't mean to startle you." The man gives me a familiar smile. Familiar, because I saw it on his faculty page less than two hours ago. It falters as he gives me a closer look. "Are you a student?"

"No."

"Then may I ask what you're looking for? There's not much down here besides me and a bunch of old rock collections."

"I'm looking for you, actually."

The smile returns, a little broader than before.

"Really? I was just on my way to my next class, but if you'd like to join me for the walk?"

"I would, thank you."

"I'm Blake Davis, but I suppose you must know that already. And you are?"

The second my mouth opens, I realize I shouldn't give him my real name. I'm not supposed to be here. I'm under a direct order not to ask questions. Having a geology professor google my name could definitely raise some alarms with the wrong people. So I say the first name that pops into my mind.

"Betty."

"What can I do for you, Betty?" he asks, holding the door to the stairwell open for me.

Our steps are so loud, I feel like I have to yell to be heard over them as I say, "I was hoping you could help answer a few questions about natural resources in South Florida."

"Well, you've found the right guy for that. Animal, mineral, or other?"

"I'm thinking mineral, but possibly other."

"Interesting. How can I help you decide?"

"I was wondering if there was anything that could be found in the area that would make properties far more valuable than they'd normally be?"

His smile remains in place, but it becomes fake, strained. His eyes harden with suspicion.

"Why would you want to know something like that?"

Trying to buy some time, I hurry up the last few risers and hit the bar on the door with both hands. Watch as he follows me somewhat reluctantly, the distrust in his expression growing.

I really should have thought this out better before I came here. If I tell him I'm investigating a crime, he might want to see identification. Mine doesn't match the name I just gave him. But if I don't think of a decent reason, he might not take me seriously. Worse, he might decide not to help me at all.

"I'm writing a book," I say, before I can think twice about it. "A murder mystery. Only, I might have written myself into a corner. I've been using the victims' properties as motive, but now that I've reached the point where I need to reveal why the properties were worth killing over, I realize that I have no idea. And I really don't want to just make something up."

"Ah, I see. And why did you originally choose to go with using the land as motive?"

It feels like a test, but considering it's the first question he's asked that I have an answer for, hopefully it's one that I'll pass.

"When I was younger, I did a report on the uranium deposits in Central Florida. I guess I figured that maybe they extended far enough south that I could use that, but it turns out that I should have checked first." I shrug and give him a bashful smile. "I was hoping that maybe, with your help, it wouldn't be too painful of a lesson to learn."

The distrust clouding his features has softened but isn't gone completely.

"Do you have a backup plan in case I'm not able to help?"

"I do, but I'd really hate to use it."

"What is it?"

"Treasure."

"You mean like gold and jewels?"

I duck my head as if with shame. "Yes."

"Yeah, you're right. It would be a shame to take that route. Especially when I have a far more valuable commodity that you can use."

"Really?"

As we step from the building, out into the stifling heat and blinding sun, I search his expression. All traces of wariness are gone. Instead, a giant smile splits his face.

"Really."

"You're a lifesaver. What is it?"

"Oil."

"Oil?" I repeat, not sure I heard him right.

"Yes. Oil."

"In South Florida?" I ask doubtfully.

"That's correct."

"Like, off the coast?"

"No. Like under the land."

I stare at him, searching for any signs that he's joking, but there are none. "That seems like something the general public would be aware of."

His grin grows even bigger. "It does, doesn't it?"

"But is it accessible? I mean, is there a reason why nobody's tried to drill for it before?"

"It is accessible. Some of the pockets have been tapped already, albeit from the water. Fortunately, there's currently a ban restricting drilling within three miles of the coast, which prevents them from accessing the deposits under the land. An excellent decision, considering one run-in with a hurricane could cause a spill that would damage the beaches for years to come. But as to why there isn't a stretch of the Tamiami that looks like the oil fields in Texas?"

My throat clicks as I try to swallow. I force myself to draw slow, deep breaths, and even then, dizziness threatens to take hold.

"I can only assume because someone would have to buy enough property from private citizens to make it feasible. And not everyone would be willing to sell. There's the motive for your book. Trust me. In this area? Oil is the best treasure you'll find."

CHAPTER 35

I pull into the parking lot of the first grocery store I come to, though I'm not in the mood to shop. I have no appetite. Can barely stomach the thought of pushing a cart down narrow aisles under the sickly glow of florescent lights, forcing myself to smile at strangers as they catch my eye.

But I feel even less like being out in the middle of the swamp right now, with no one but myself to tell me that the noise I just heard was the wind. A branch. Paranoia. Because even if I am being paranoid, it's not like I don't have good cause.

At the end of the day, there's someone who's taken at least two lives and they're still out there. It could be a friend. A neighbor. An experienced assassin. The point is, it could be anyone.

And I have what they want. Me and no one else. At least, no one who's still alive. It's a precarious position to be in. I know I'll have to go back to the sanctuary eventually, just… not yet.

So I exit my car and make my way inside. Get a cart and walk the aisles. Pretend that it matters what brand of orange juice I get, that I'm looking forward to eating the comfort foods I grab, even though the potato chips and cookies hold no appeal. And when I make it to the far end of the store, I walk back to the entrance and start again.

I've almost completed my second lap when the ding of an incoming alert sounds from my pocket. It's the noise I chose for the security app. Specifically, the tone to let me know when a human image has been detected by one of the cameras.

Telling myself it's a false alarm, I pull my phone out. Wake the device with trembling fingers. Look at the image on the screen, feeling dizzy with relief when I recognize Alicia standing on the front doorstep.

As I watch, she looks at her own phone. A moment later, the cell in my hand buzzes with an incoming text from my new friend.

Hey, I'm at UR place. Will U B home soon?

I debate a moment before answering.

Not for a while. What's up?

A GIF of a sad dog appears.

Just thought U might want company.

Definitely! Are you free later this afternoon?

Would 3 work?

Sounds perfect!

Great! C U then!

I'm pocketing my phone when it buzzes again. I smile to myself, imagining what Alicia's going to add, but the new message isn't from her. It's from Jake.

Do you like Chinese food?

Is this a trick question?

No.

Then yes.

Would you like Chinese food tonight? There's a good place near where I work. I can grab some on my way over later?

The idea of eating anything right now makes my stomach recoil. I start asking for a raincheck, then reconsider. What if this is a date? After the way we left things last night, it could be. Either way, as much as I don't want food right now, I do want company. So I change my answer.

Sounds great.

And as I slip my phone back into my pocket, I realize that it really does. What I need is a distraction while waiting to hear from Director Jacobson. Now I have two. It's a relief to know that I'm not facing this alone, even if I can't tell anyone else what's going on.

At the very least, there are people who will notice I'm missing if something happens to me. At the most? I feel a blush spreading across my cheeks as I think about Jake, pushing my cart toward the checkout. The cashier gives me a big smile as I place my items on the conveyor belt.

"You look happy," she comments. "Having a good day?"

"You know, it didn't start out that way, but I think it's going to be."

We make small talk as she rings up my purchases. On impulse, I throw a candy bar in among the rest of the items, my appetite suddenly back. As soon as I'm out of the store, I open the wrapper and take a big bite, humming to myself while I chew on my way to the car.

Even the ring of my phone doesn't spoil my mood. And when I spot who it is, I suspect my day just got even better.

"Mallory?"

"Hey, Cassidy. Listen, sorry it took me so long to get back to you. I wasn't ignoring you. Honest."

"There's no need to apologize. *I'm* the one who asked *you* for a favor."

"Yeah, but I should have called before now, regardless. Checked to see how you were doing."

"Well, you're calling now. So what have you got

for me?”

My phone beeps as another call comes through. Not recognizing the number, I send it to voicemail.

“Probably not nearly as much as you want,” she says. “It’s been crazy hard finding anything about these Myers and Kleinman guys. Who are they, anyway?”

“Possibly no one.”

“Yeah, well, they’ve piqued my curiosity, so they’re in for it now. Especially since I’ve found out who the key players are.”

“You have?”

My phone beeps again. Same number. I ignore it again, hoping the caller will take the hint and leave a message.

“Intel on all the employees I’ve been able to sniff out so far should be hitting your inbox now.”

“Mallory, you’re amazing!”

“I know. And I’m going to keep digging. Something tells me I’ve barely scratched the surface.” A third beep interrupts what she’s saying. “—don’t trust anyone who works this hard to keep their secrets.”

“They wouldn’t even let me in the building without an appointment,” I tell her. “Not even to make one.”

“Seriously? That’s shady.”

“Right?”

There’s a pause before she responds. Her voice is much softer as she says, “How are you really doing, Cass?”

“I’m… fine.”

“Really?”

“Yes. I mean, I’m not going to lie. It was tough for a while there, but I’m doing better. Each day is getting easier.”

As I say it, I realize it’s true. Despite what’s been

going on, the anxiety that had felt so crippling when I first came down here has loosened its hold on me. So have the panic attacks. I feel almost normal again. At least, as normal as I ever feel.

"You know if you ever need to talk, you can give me a call, right?"

"I do. Thanks, Mallory. For everything. I really appreciate it."

I end the call, immediately besieged by the same unfamiliar number that kept interrupting my conversation with Mallory. Whoever it is, they're relentless. It's clear that they aren't going to stop until I answer. So I do.

"Hello?"

"Don't say anything. Buy a burner phone and call me back at this number. Make sure you're somewhere safe. Outside. Private but well populated."

With that, the line goes dead. The anxiety I thought was in my past is back in an instant, even stronger than it was before. Because I'm fairly certain that was Director Jacobson. And she sounded terrified.

CHAPTER 36

I call from a disposable Motorola that I paid for with cash at a gas station. When Director Jacobson picks up, it sounds like there's water running in the background, like she's answered the phone while taking a shower.

"Where are you?" I ask.

"Never mind about that. Where are *you*? Are you somewhere safe?"

"I'm in the parking lot of the tourist center on the Tamiami."

"How many people are there?"

"About four dozen? Maybe five? None within fifty feet of me."

"Good. Now how soon can you get out of there?"

"I'm about a two-minute walk from my car."

"I meant Florida."

"What's going on?" I ask, wondering if there's something I've missed. A case so big that all hands have been called on deck. But that wouldn't explain why she wanted me to buy a burner phone. Why she called me from an unfamiliar number. Or why she's acting so strangely. "Are you okay?"

"I'm fine… for now."

"I don't understand."

"You don't need to. There'll be time to explain things later, but right now, I just need to know that you're on your way to somewhere else. Is there a bus station nearby?"

"A—no, I have my car."

"Leave it."

Director Jacobson's breath heaves on the other end of the line, a big wavering sigh that makes goosebumps rise on my skin. I've never heard her like this before. She's always been so calm. So rational. Even when my partner was killed, she barely showed emotion, somehow keeping her stoic façade in place.

But now? She doesn't sound like her usual self. She's barely making sense.

"I need you to listen very carefully," she says. "I've been told to leave this alone."

"Leave what alone? Me?"

"No. Whatever's going on in your hometown. Whatever happened to Tortoise Trails. Turtle Glen. Whatever you want to call it."

"It's oil," I say, swallowing hard. "I don't know about any of the other locations, but that's why they want the land here."

She curses. "No wonder they want me to back off."

"Who's they?"

"The top. That's all you need to know."

But it's not. The top could mean anyone from the director of the FBI to the president of the United States.

"Who did you tell?" I ask.

"That's just it. No one. I've been handling this on my own, haven't discussed this with anyone besides you."

"Then how—?"

"I don't know. Not exactly. Every single search I've done has been using my encrypted computer at the Bureau. It should have been secure. Which means we've either been hacked, which we'd know by now, or I triggered some kind of internal search filter that was already in place."

A shrill shriek splits the air. I jump, heart thudding violently in my chest as I scan the parking lot, searching for the source.

"Cassidy! Are you all right? Are you there?" Director Jacobson asks, her voice high-pitched.

"It was just a kid," I say, though the knowledge brings no solace.

"You need to lay low for a while. Don't let me know where you're going. Don't let me know when you get there. Ditch your cell phone now. Dump it in the bed of some tourist's truck. I'll call you on this number in a few days and give you an update. We'll figure out where to go from there."

"I can't leave," I say.

"Listen, Cassidy. I know you've had an impossibly rough few weeks. That you're grieving. That your grandfather's been murdered and you want to find his killer. That's commendable. Really. But you need to walk away."

"I don't think I can."

"You have to."

I shake my head even though she can't see me. It's my fault she's in this mess. It's what I do—put the people I care about at risk. But it ends now. "I'm staying."

"You're being an idiot."

"I know. But if it's this big, they're going to find me anyway."

"That's not true."

"I can't hide indefinitely."

"There are… options."

"And there's CCTV. Face recognition software.

Voice identification programs. I can't stay off the grid forever. If someone wants to find me, it's going to happen."

"I can figure this out. I just need more time."

"No." I swallow hard. Blink away the tears forming in my eyes. "You're the one who needs to walk away. From this. From me. No sneaking around trying to find out who's behind the mask. Make it clear that you don't care. That you're done looking."

"You don't mean that."

"I do," I say. "You have to. It might be the only way either of us survives this. Start filing the paperwork to terminate my employment. Attribute it to mental issues. Dr. Parsons already suggested I was delusional. Go with that. I'll make sure to sell it on my end, too. Do my best to make sure no one takes anything I say seriously. Maybe—"

My voice cracks. I draw a deep breath and try again.

"Maybe it'll be enough. If I'm not a threat, maybe I won't be worth their effort. Maybe they'll worry that if something does happen to me, people will start thinking twice about the crazy stuff I was saying to see if there was some credibility to it."

"Those are really big maybes."

"I understand that. But the decision's been made. This is the way it has to be."

A sniff comes from the other end of the line. "There's nothing I can do to make you reconsider, is there?"

"There's not."

"Then I guess all there is for me to say is good luck. If you change your mind, if you need *anything*, you let me know, okay? We'll figure a way out of this."

"Thank you."

"And Agent Knox?"

I almost don't hear her, already ending the call. Pressing the phone back against my ear, I ask, "Yes?"

"We didn't keep you out of the field so long because we didn't believe in you. It's just… most of the other agents? They don't have a mind like yours. They can't do what you do, spotting patterns where only one or two faint threads exist. Maybe we were being selfish, but we were trying to keep you safe because you're irreplaceable. We needed you. We still do. If there's a moment where you have to make a tough choice, I want you to remember that."

And then she's gone. I'm alone in a parking lot full of tourists who think the alligators are the most dangerous thing here. But they're not. I am. Let's just hope my adversaries don't know it yet.

CHAPTER 37

I remember reading once about elephants. I was amazed to learn about their exceptional memories. Touched to discover that they made pilgrimages to visit the bones of deceased family members to mourn them. But what surprised me most of all were the tales of vengeance.

It's not lost on me why this memory is surfacing now as I drive back to the sanctuary. Neither is the fact that I may never get the chance to put my plan into action. I may get struck down first. But if I'm not, it doesn't matter how long I have to wait. I'm going to find out who killed my grandfather. And I'm going to make them pay.

But if I even hope to have that opportunity, I'm going to have to be smart about it. Which is why I pull over onto the side of the road as soon as the driveway comes into view ahead.

I dig around for my phone, the real one, so I can check the surveillance cameras, make sure no one's there waiting for me. Ignore the little voice in my head whispering that if whatever shadowy faction that's behind this have infiltrated the FBI, then they can surely manage to alter my video feeds, because I have to do *something* to make myself believe I have a fighting chance.

Even if it's a lie.

Pressing my thumb to the sensor, I wake the screen. Scroll through the list of notifications, dismissing them one by one until there's something that catches my eye. The email from Mallory containing what she'd been able to uncover so far about Myers and Kleinman.

I glance around at the empty road. It's not like I'm in any kind of rush. I might as well see what she discovered.

Opening the email, I find three words: More to come. That's it besides two PDF attachments. Opening the first, I find a bunch of screenshots pasted into the document. The social media posts, newspaper blurbs, and publicity releases that provided Mallory with the names to use for her search. I exit out and access the second file.

At the top are two obituaries, one for Kleinman and one for Myers. Both of the founding partners passed away almost a decade ago. Since then, the firm has been kept alive by Kleinman's daughter, Jessica, a sour-faced woman who looks to be somewhere in her mid-sixties, and a number of partners.

I don't take the time to read the biography Mallory created for each of them. For now, I just skim their faces, looking for someone familiar. But when I find the photograph of one who is, I wish I hadn't.

I suck in a sharp breath, feeling gut punched. Enlarge the image on the screen, sure I must be mistaken. Harden my stomach against the surge of queasiness as I realize I'm not. I press my lips into a tight line to quell their trembling, but it doesn't help.

Returning to the home screen on my phone, I find the number in my contacts and tap the call button. The nails of my free hand dig deep into my palm while I wait for the call to connect. I've been such a fool.

"Hey, I was just getting ready to call you. I forgot

to ask—are you more of a moo shu pork fan or a beef and broccoli kind of girl?"

The statement I answer with isn't what he's looking for.

"You work for Myers and Kleinman. No, scratch that. You don't just work there, you're one of the partners, which means you help run the place."

"Who told you that?"

"Are you going to deny it?"

Squeezing my eyes shut, I pray that he does. His silence dashes my hopes—and ignites my fury.

"How long did you think you could keep this from me?"

"Cassie—"

"When I mentioned them to you, when I told you my concerns, you dismissed them. You made me feel ridiculous about my suspicions. And now I know why. Because it might cost your company a couple of dollars if I run my mouth and cause them bad press."

"That's not it."

"Then why? What are you trying to hide? What was Butch's connection to the company?"

"There was no connection. I drew up the will as a favor. It was never on the books. As far as I know, they aren't aware he existed."

"So they didn't want his property?"

"No."

"And they didn't have him killed?"

"*No.*"

"Did you kill him?"

"What? No! I would never. Cassie, you know how I felt about Butch."

His voice breaks. I swallow hard, reminding myself that the man I'm speaking with is a liar. I shouldn't trust him, and I certainly shouldn't feel bad for him.

"You know what my situation was like growing up. Everyone did." Though it's spoken barely above a whisper, each word rings loud in my ears, because it's true. "If it hadn't been for Butch—I owe everything to your grandfather. If it hadn't been for him, who knows what would have happened to me. He taught me to be the man I am today. How to be a *good* man."

"Then why did you lie to me?"

"I don't know. I guess, at first, I just wanted a chance for us to get to know each other again. I wanted you to like me for me, not because—"

"Because you were a hotshot lawyer rolling in money? If you knew me at all, you'd realize that was a strike against you, not for you."

"I do know you, Cassie. And I knew you'd feel that way. And I knew I'd end up telling you the truth behind why I work there, and I didn't want *that* affecting the way you felt about me."

"And what's the truth? That you're a good person who just so happens to work for a bad company?"

"Yes."

I hadn't been expecting him to admit it. I chew on the inside of my cheek, forcing myself to stay silent.

"I'm not going to lie. At first, I liked working there. The prestige of it. Having people look at me like I was worth something. Not being swamp scum anymore."

I remember my own confession I'd made to Jake. It's the very same reason I'd given for why I dated Matt in high school.

"And it was easy. I was good at it. Most of the time it was mediating between two whiny rich guys while they battled over a company, or power. But then I started to see the bigger picture. That maybe the guy I represented would treat his employees worse than the other one did. Or he was only going after the company so he could shut it down, use it as a tax write-off, and all the hardworking people who depended on that company would be out of a job."

"Then why did you stay?"

"Because if I didn't do it, someone else would. And at least if it was me, I could use the money I made off them for good."

"So it *was* about the money."

He swallows so loudly I can hear it over the phone. I listen as he draws a shaky breath. "Have you thought about how you're going to keep the sanctuary open?" he asks.

"What's that got to do with anything?"

"Have you?"

"The same way that Butch did."

"Then it's still about the money."

"What are you saying?"

"Have you bothered to look at any of Butch's accounts yet?" When I don't answer, he says, "I'll save you the trouble. They're empty."

"What do you mean?"

Jake sighs heavily. "Butch almost lost the sanctuary about ten years ago. I only found out because one of my jobs back then at the firm was to look at tax liens, foreclosures, companies that were in distress, that kind of thing."

"And the sanctuary?"

"Was in foreclosure."

"Why didn't Butch ever mention it?"

"He never said anything to me, either. You know how proud he was. And you also know that place was his life. Losing it would have destroyed him. So I've done what I've had to over the years."

"Which is?"

"Falsifying documents that the sanctuary was the benefactor of someone's will. Creating fake companies that give regular donations. Paying bills before they ever made their way to Butch for him to see. Take your pick."

"But all of the money was really from you?"

"Yes."

"And he never knew?"

"No."

I dig my fists into my eyes, trying to crush the tears. "So when you promised Butch you'd help me, you were intending to keep these secret contributions going?"

"I still will, Cassie. It's the reason why I work at Myers and Kleinman today. The only reason."

"If all that's true, what was in the sealed envelope in Butch's will? The one with his contingency plan if I didn't want to keep the sanctuary?"

"It doesn't matter now because you're staying, right?"

"What did it say?" After a long pause, I add, "If you were his lawyer, you know. So what was it?"

His voice is low as he admits, "If you didn't want it, he was leaving it to me."

"Well, you're off the hook. On all accounts. Your assistance is no longer necessary in any form."

"Cassie, can we please talk about this?"

"We just did."

I hang up. My throat is painfully tight, breath hitching as I finally release the tears I worked so hard to hold back. The phone rings in my clenched fist as Jake calls back. I power the device off so I won't be tempted to answer.

This is for the best. It had to be done. The only way to keep him safe is to cut ties. I just wish it wasn't so hard to hate him.

CHAPTER 38

Pulling back onto the road, I drive the last mile to the sanctuary, turning into the driveway without bothering to check the surveillance camera feeds. What's the point? I've already lost so much, more than I can even process right now. I already feel defeated.

All I want to do is go inside, curl up in a ball, and hibernate. I don't have any more fight left in me today.

Even just hauling myself out of the car feels like a monumental task. My shoes drag through the dirt, raising puffs of dust as I trudge to the front door. I'm digging the keys out of my purse when I hear the crunch of tires on gravel.

Closing my eyes, I curse. It's not that I didn't know what it meant, when I decided not to flee. I guess I just thought I'd have more time to prepare before everything came to a head. But evil doesn't take a raincheck.

Unlocking the door, I linger outside, waiting as the sound of the engine grows louder. As the black truck emerges from the trees, pulling up behind me. As Gordon climbs down from the cab. I guess it's time.

My gaze drifts over his shoulder to the barn, to where the pitchfork leans against the outer wall. I really should have learned to put that thing away by now. Or to keep it with me at all times. One or the other, because seeing it now, so far out of reach, is an odd form of torture.

Sighing, I head inside without a word. Spin and wait for Gordon to join me.

"Hey," he says, blinking rapidly as his eyes adjust from the brightness of the sun to the dim interior of the house. "How's it going?"

I don't respond, just stare at him instead. Feel a small twinge of satisfaction as he shifts uneasily, tugging at his shirt collar.

"Listen, about the other day. I should apologize."

"For what?" I ask, silently listing his string of offenses in my mind, wondering which he'll choose.

"Well, um, I guess for the way I behaved? I didn't mean to come off as judgmental."

"Then what did you mean to come off as?"

"I can see you're still upset."

"I'm just tired of everyone sidestepping the real issue."

"Which is?"

"Why are you really here, Gordon? Is it to find out if I'm ready to sell yet?"

The corners of his mouth edge up in a smile. "Are you?"

"No." Crossing my arms over my chest, I look him in the eye and say, "I've decided to stay."

His face clouds over. "You don't want to do that."

I can't resist laughing. "As strange as it might seem, I do."

He takes a step forward, then another, his movements slow and calculated, like a panther stalking its prey, continuing to approach until he's standing way too close to me, well within my personal space. I force myself to stand my ground, refusing to cede an inch.

"Trust me. You really don't."

My hand brushes my side, where my firearm should be. But it's not. It's still in an evidence box somewhere in Virginia, a casualty of the last man who made the mistake of underestimating me.

Gordon flexes his fingers, curls them into fists. I imagine how good my own would feel curled into a fist around the grip of a gun. A memory of Butch's old revolver in the box in my closet comes to mind, how familiar it had looked against its soft foam bedding, as much an old friend as the one looming before me.

I'd been reluctant to so much as think of holding a gun again after what happened to my partner, as if seeing the destruction wrought by such a thing had shocked me into some form of non-violence. It seems silly now. And as I see myself in my mind's eye pick up a weapon and aim it at the man before me, I find it's an affliction that I no longer suffer from.

"I think you should leave," I say.

"And I *know* you should," he counters.

"What's going on here?"

I glance up, surprised to see Alicia standing in the doorway.

"Gordon was just leaving."

"That's a good idea," she says, storming across the room to my side.

Gordon's dark eyes narrow as he gives me a look that makes the skin on the back of my neck quiver. "This isn't over."

"Uh, yeah, I think it is," Alicia says, giving him a pointed scowl. Her shoulder brushes against mine as he turns to leave, her long hair tickling my arm as we watch him disappear over the threshold.

I step forward and give the door a kick, slamming it shut behind him.

"Ugh, what a creeper," she says.

I bite my tongue before I can respond. If she only knew how right she was, she'd probably regret what she just did. Hopefully I can get this situation under control one way or another before the decision catches up with her.

CHAPTER 39

Alicia turns to face me, her gaze so searching as she looks me up and down that it feels like the gentle tug of Velcro against my skin. I do my best to ignore the sensation, forcing a smile I don't feel. Her expression lets me know she doesn't buy it.

"You look like you could use a drink."

"That's all right. I—"

"You sit." She pulls a bottle of wine from her oversized handbag and sets it on the coffee table. I stare at the strap as she adjusts it on her shoulder, feeling something tug at my memory as she says, "I'll get us some glasses."

I need to keep my senses sharp. Alcohol isn't the answer. I sink onto the couch anyway, because it's not worth arguing over. Immediately I scoot to the edge of the cushion to stand and help as I realize she doesn't know her way around.

But as I watch her reflection in the TV screen, she walks straight to the middle cabinet and opens the lefthand side—the one that several wineglasses call home. How does she know that?

"Did Gordon just show up?" she asks.

"Yeah. He's still trying to talk me into selling the property."

"Really?"

"

She pulls out the drawer where Butch kept the corkscrew. I slide to the far end of the couch and look out the window where a black truck is parked. Not Jake's. Or Gordon's. Hers.

I'd been so eager to make a new friend, so desperate, that I've overlooked things I should have paid attention to. Some of those threads that Director Jacobson credited me with being so good at spotting. And now that I'm looking, there are plenty.

Alicia's enthusiasm to befriend me when the girl I was familiar with wouldn't have given me the time of day. Her vehicle matching the description of the one seen outside Grace Billie's house the night she was killed. The way she tried to convince me that Jake was trouble, and that Gordon was harmless. Even the way Gordon had backed down just now when she'd given the order.

Though it's just a guess, I ask, "How long have you and he worked together?"

"He told you that?"

"Yes," I lie.

I can just barely hear as she mutters the word *idiot*.

"What got him so PO'd, anyway?" she asks instead of answering. "I don't think I've ever seen him like that."

"I told him that I've decided to stay."

Her reflection in the TV screen stops moving. Her head turns slowly in my direction. I can feel her eyes boring a hole into the back of my head.

"Is that so?" she asks, her voice low and measured.

I glance toward the bedroom down the hall, twenty feet away.

"It is."

"Well, like I told your grandfather, it's a gorgeous

piece of land."

I watch as she fingers her purse strap, a one-inch band of leather. I bet it's a perfect match to the ligature mark around Butch's neck. And that slider on the strap she just adjusted? It looks like the same shape and size as the anomaly in his bruise.

Plus, I distinctly remember her saying she'd never met my grandfather before. Only she just admitted to speaking to him. I may have been blind before, but my eyes are wide open now. This woman is Butch's killer, and I suspect she intends for me to be her next victim.

"Where are you going?" she asks as I stand.

"To the bathroom." I force a casual grin and gesture to the wine on the table. "I need to make room before we drink that."

She studies my face. "No, I don't think so."

I laugh, playing stupid, and move toward the hall. "I'll be right back. I promise, you won't even have time to miss me."

The hair on my arms bristles as I turn my back on her.

"I said no."

The unmistakable sound of a gun cocking seems deafeningly loud in the silent room. I spin around to find myself staring at the barrel of a pistol.

"You couldn't just leave and make things easy, could you?" She keeps the weapon aimed at me, entering the living room. Smartly, she gives me a wide berth, keeping the couch between us.

"Why'd you do it?" I ask. "Why'd you kill Butch?"

"It's quite simple, really. Because he had something I wanted."

"The land?"

Alicia nods.

"And Grace?" I prod.

"Same thing. We made them both generous offers."

"Who's we?"

The smile she gives me makes my skin crawl. "That doesn't matter."

I laugh.

"You don't even know, do you?" I ask.

But she doesn't take the bait.

"I know that Butch and Grace should have been smart enough to take it."

"But they weren't."

"No," she says, throwing her hands up in frustration. Immediately, she trains the barrel of her weapon back on me. "It's swamp land," she sneers. "It's certainly not worth dying over. And yet…" She shrugs.

"But it's worth killing over," I say.

"Not the land. But the oil beneath it is."

I take a step away from her.

"Stop moving," she growls.

Ignoring the order, I take another step backwards.

"The last thing I need is a mess to clean up, but I will shoot you."

Eyeing the space between us, I think, *you'll shoot* at *me*. The question is if she's a good enough shot to hit me. I've seen enough law enforcement officers just barely pass their firearms qualifications to be willing to take my chances. I hold eye contact, careful not to betray what I'm thinking, not wanting to give her warning that I'm about to bolt.

But just as I'm about to make my move, there's a knock on the door. The handle twists. It cracks open.

I don't know who it is, but I have to warn them.

"She has a gun," I yell. "Run."

But I'm too late. Jake's head is already inside. "Cassie?"

His eyes widen as he sees the weapon pointed at him. He goes visibly pale.

Alicia might not be able to make a kill shot from twenty feet away, but it would be hard to miss from five.

His gaze shifts from Alicia to me as he steps inside, closing the door behind him.

"You okay?" he asks me.

I was, but now? I nod, even though I'm not.

Alicia smirks, gesturing for Jake to come closer. When he doesn't, she extends her gun arm, the barrel of the pistol now less than three feet from his head.

"I'll tell you what we're going to do here," she says. "I'm going to give you some paperwork and you're going to sign it."

I bob my head, signaling agreeance.

"Yeah, of course."

She snorts and rolls her eyes.

"Then you're both going to text your employers and tell them you quit. That the two of you are running off together."

I look at Jake instead of her, trying to convey how sorry I am that he became a part of this mess.

"Then the three of us are going for a little drive."

I know where she's going to take us. Alligator Alley. And like the hundreds of bodies that have been dumped there before us, we won't be coming back. I can't let this get that far.

Never let your abductor take you to a secondary location. It's violent crime survival 101.

If she kills us here, there will be evidence. The sheriff might not be bright enough to find it, but at least there's a chance she won't get away with it.

"Fine," I say. I move closer, stop when I see the

look Jake's giving me. I glance at Alicia, but she hasn't noticed, no doubt enjoying my anguish too much. My lips tremble as I look back at Jake.

One, he mouths.

I move my head slightly to the left, then to the right. A shake. No.

He nods yes and mouths *two*.

Tears spill from my eyes, searing hot as they hit my cheeks. He's too close. It's too risky. I can't do this. Yet if I don't act when Jake does whatever it is he has planned, we both might die.

Three.

Like a striking snake his hand flashes out, shoving Alicia's arm up. The gun fires, drywall raining from the ceiling. I don't stick around to find out what happens next. I can't.

The sounds of them wrestling over the weapon chase me as I run down the hall and dart into the bedroom. Snatching the box from the shelf in the closet, I grab the rusty key from my nightstand and work it in the ancient lock. For a long, breathless moment, it doesn't turn. I jiggle it sideways, the inner mechanism clicking as it finally gives, turning to the side.

In an instant I flip the lid open and snatch the revolver from inside, just as Alicia's gun fires again. Praying I'm not too late, I dash back into the hall, staying low as I approach the living room.

I don't see Jake, but it doesn't take much detective skill to deduce that he's what Alicia is aiming at, her mouth twisted in a nasty smile as she extends the gun toward a target on the floor.

"Freeze," I yell. "FBI. Alicia Harris, you are under ar—"

But she doesn't even seem to hear me. Her finger twitches, tightening, curling as she moves to pull the trigger. I know the bullets will travel the distance between us in a blink, but will it be fast enough? I fire two shots in quick succession as I run forward.

Alicia spins in my direction, the pistol in her hand now pointed at me. I zig to the side, bouncing off the wall, but it's unnecessary. My aim was true, my shots clean, the bullets entering straight through one ear and out the other, lodging in the blood-spattered molding beside the front door.

I watch as her body slumps to the floor. It's so quiet that the sounds of my labored breathing, my thundering pulse, my hard swallow, are the only things I hear. My progress toward the living room slows, afraid of what I might find when I get there.

"Jake?" I call, my voice shaking as I shove the revolver into the back of my waistband.

"Yeah?"

He sounds weak, but he's alive. I hurry forward, pausing only to snatch Alicia's weapon from her limp outstretched hand before collapsing to my knees beside him where he sits propped against the couch.

A red stain grows on his shirt. I push my palm firmly against the hole in his left shoulder. He winces with a hiss. I ignore it, taking stock of the injury, probing his anatomy with my other hand. The entrance wound is just below the end of his clavicle.

I pull his shirt up, tugging it over his good arm, then his head. Use the fabric to keep pressure on his wound as I ease him forward and take a look at where the bullet exited. And then I breathe.

It's a clean through-and-through, small caliber bullet, no ballooning on the exit. He should be okay. I sigh deeply with relief as I gently lower him back against the front of the couch. Though his skin is grey and coated with sweat, he's giving me a lopsided grin.

“What?” I ask.

“There are easier ways to get me to take my shirt off, you know.”

CHAPTER 40

Those few brief moments when I thought Jake might be dead were agony. Images of us as children flashed through my mind. Laughing hysterically over jokes only we understood. Holding hands while we ran through the sprinklers. The kiss I'd planted on his cheek after my five-year-old self told him he was going to be my husband one day. The beaming smile he'd given me in return.

When I heard Jake's voice, when I saw with my own eyes that he was alive, well, there's no way to describe the feelings that went through me. It didn't matter that adult Jake had been less than honest with me. That there was so much I didn't know about him. That he had a special knack for crawling under my skin, driving me insane the way no other human on this planet can.

Somehow, the man before me was both the boy who had been my best friend and a stranger, and yet there was one thing they both had in common—I wanted them in my life.

There's never been anyone who made me feel like he has, both the good and the bad. True, things could go horribly, terribly wrong between us. But if it worked? It could be magic.

How could I turn my back on that? I'm not sure

it would be possible, even if I tried.

"Can you walk?" I ask, helping him to his feet.

He winces, gritting his jaw against the pain he's in, but says, "Yeah."

"Good. Get in the car. I'll be there in a minute."

I grab a couple of clean towels and a roll of gauze from the bathroom, then hurry back down the hall to the living room. Pause as I pass Alicia on my way out the front door. A stack of papers sticks out from the edge of her purse. Leaning closer, I see the documents she wanted me to sign, the ones to sell the property.

Snatching them free, I rush outside, not bothering to lock the door. Tossing the papers on the back seat, I hand Jake the towels. He drapes one over the passenger seat and takes a seat while I rip open the gauze and tie the end in a knot.

"Lean forward," I say. He eyes me warily, for good cause. This is going to hurt. A lot.

He lets loose with a string of obscenities as I pack the wound on his back. By the time I'm done, he's panting, drenched in sweat, his jaw clenched tight. He holds up a hand as I move toward the entry hole made by the bullet.

"Please. Don't."

"You promise to keep pressure on it the whole way there?" I ask. "We've got a long drive and I don't want you bleeding out on the way to the hospital."

He nods, pressing the second towel to his shoulder. I lean over him, buckle his seatbelt, then jog to the driver's side and get behind the wheel. Cranking the engine, I throw the car in gear and speed up the driveway. Pull out my cell phone and dial, switching the call over to Bluetooth as I turn onto the road.

Alicia may be dead, but that doesn't mean the danger is gone. Taking her life will place me right in the center of the radar of whoever she worked for. But maybe there's a way to get ahead of the fallout and take charge. The ringing stops as the call is answered.

"Agent Knox?"

Director Jacobson sounds spooked. Worried. And it's no wonder. It's been less than two hours since we last spoke, though it seems much longer. Not to mention I called her normal number from my normal number. She must think I lost it.

"Director Jacobson, please, just listen. I need your help. I shot a woman. Killed her. Her name is Alicia Harris. She admitted to killing my grandfather and a neighbor, Grace Billie, because they wouldn't agree to sell her their land."

I can feel Jake staring at me from the passenger seat, but I don't let that distract me. I only have one chance to get this right. If Director Jacobson is correct, if one or both of our phones has been compromised— and right now, I really hope that they have—there might be a way to salvage this situation.

"She was working with a local real estate agent named Gordon Massey. I know him from school, he'd been trying to convince me to sell to a developer friend of his. I don't know how much he knows, or who the developer is, but it appears as if Alicia was falsifying documents, creating fake buyers and investors on the purchase agreements."

There's a long pause while I try to think of anything else I should add, but when in doubt, keep it simple. I've laid all the blame on Alicia. Made it clear that I don't know who else is involved. Created plausible deniability for her associates. There's not much else I can do.

"Are you okay?" Director Jacobson asks.

"Yes, but my friend isn't. He's been shot. We're

on the way to the hospital now. I haven't called the police to report what happened yet. There was no time to wait for them to arrive, or an ambulance. We're half an hour out from the nearest medical facility and he is losing blood too fast."

"Don't worry about that. I'll call the local authorities and fill them in on what's going on."

"My grandfather's murder, and Grace's, are being investigated by Detective Miguel Torres with the state police."

"Then that's who I'll call."

"Thank you."

"And Agent Knox?"

"Yes?"

"Good work. And good luck."

The call ends, the car falling silent besides the hum of the wheels traveling much too fast across the concrete. Then, from the passenger seat, "You were right."

I glance over at Jake. His head is pressed back against the seat, eyes shut. He looks way too pale, and shaky, and like he might be sick.

"It's okay."

"But it's not. Are Myers and Kleinman involved?"

"I don't think that they are."

"But you don't know for sure."

I reach over and take his hand. Give it a squeeze.

"It's over," I tell him. And I pray that it's true.

CHAPTER 41

Though it's late, well after dark by the time I arrive back home, the sanctuary is still a flurry of activity. My hands tense on the steering wheel as I drive past the flashing lights and commotion on the way to the barn, averting my gaze from the two black trucks parked in front of the house. One of their owners is never coming to collect it. The other nearly met the same fate.

I remind myself to breathe as I think about Jake. Though visiting hours were over by the time he was out of surgery, after the doctor found me in the waiting room to give me an update, I managed to talk her into letting me see him before I left.

He'd been sleeping, still under the effects of the anesthesia. I used the opportunity to study him while his guard was down—the hard line of his stubbled jaw, the soft purse of his lips, his tanned skin bleached colorless by blood loss.

It gave me a chance to reconcile the man with the little boy I used to know. I could still spot traces of him, and yet, it's not my old friend I see when I look at Jake now.

There's no denying that things between us have changed. But I'm starting to suspect that some aspects of our relationship never will.

It might have been more than three decades since

he was a daily part of my life, but the place he used to occupy is still there, waiting. And as much as I'm scared to admit it, I want him back in it. When I thought I'd lost him… I gulp a deep breath and swallow hard as I park my car and get out.

A hungry cow lows mournfully from the dark paddock. A pig squeals. Daisy snorts as I enter the barn and flick the lights on.

Immediately there's a bump and a thud, Stephano jumping over his stall door and landing on the dirt of the aisle. I'm really going to have to find a way to keep him in, for his own safety. But in the meantime, I scoop him up, cradling the goat in my arms as I drop my face against his rough coat.

I don't have all the answers. I don't know how much danger I'm in. But this life here, in Gator Glade, is worth fighting for. And that's exactly what I'm going to do.

Because it's more than just Jake. It's this place.

Since I've been here, I feel like I could be all right again. For the first time since I escaped that basement, I actually believe that I could regain everything I lost.

My confidence. My sense of safety. My independence.

I should have known that this was what I needed. The sanctuary. The spot that's always been, and always will be, my true home.

Setting Stephano down, I get to work bringing all the animals in, feeding them, getting them settled for the night. I've just finished making sure they all have fresh water when a voice shatters the peaceful sounds of them eating.

"*You're* FBI?"

It's spoken like an accusation. I continue what I'm doing, take my time rolling the hose up and hanging it on its hook on the wall before I turn to face Sheriff Kingston and say, "I am."

"You didn't think that was something you should have told me?"

"Why? Would it have made a difference?"

"It might have."

"And now?"

"When are you going home?"

Crossing my arms over my chest, I raise my eyebrows and give him the same smile you'd give a parent who's letting their child create unchecked chaos in public.

"This *is* home."

"You know what I mean."

"I do. And I'm telling you. I don't have plans to leave any time soon."

"Gonna be hard to keep your job way down here."

I shrug. "I appreciate your concern, but I'm not worried about it."

"That hoodlum you've been keeping time with isn't worth it."

I want to tell him that "hoodlum" is a high-powered lawyer, but I don't. That's Jake's secret to share. If he's kept it to himself, I can only assume he has his reasons. Besides, he deserves to be there to see the look of shock that's sure to be on Kingston's face if and when the man finds out.

Instead, I ask, "Why are you here?"

He gestures with a thumb over his shoulder toward the house. "Just because you're a Fed doesn't mean you don't have to answer for the mess you made."

Closing my eyes, I try drawing upon the well of inner strength I keep assuring myself I have, but it's run dry. It's been a long day. I've been over what happened time and time again as I sat in the hospital waiting room talking to the state police. I don't have the energy or the patience to do it again.

"I've already given my statement."

"Not to me you haven't."

"Well, I guess it's a good thing it isn't your case, then."

The sheriff's eyes narrow. He hooks his thumbs into his belt, his right hand resting on his holstered gun. "You seem to have forgotten that this is my town."

"And this is my property. It's time for you to leave."

"Listen, missy—"

"No, you listen, Lyle."

His head jerks back on his neck, his mouth tightening into a hard line. It's obvious he's not happy about me using his first name. Well, too bad.

I'm not a kid anymore. And I'm not about to let him try to intimidate me.

I've met real monsters. This man before me? He's an annoying gnat who mistakenly thinks he won't get swatted.

"You and I both know the law. This barn is not part of the crime scene. You don't have a right to be here. No amount of bullying is going to change that. So go."

"You're making a mighty big mistake."

"As long as you and your son stay off my property, I don't think that I am."

Even as I say it, I know it's not true. Petty men like Lyle Kingston don't like being reminded of the limitations to their power. They can't be trusted. There's no way he's not going to try and retaliate. But that's a problem future me will have to deal with.

He gives me a filthy look before turning and slinking toward the exit. Pausing at the doorway, he says,

"FBI or not, I don't trust you. You shouldn't have come back."

And then he's gone.

Tugging my phone from my pocket, I bring up the security app and check that the encounter recorded. Then I email a copy of the video to both my personal and work accounts. If he's smart, he'll swallow his pride and leave me alone. But if he wants a fight, I'll be waiting. And I'll be ready.

CHAPTER 42

Butterflies dance in my stomach as I pull into a spot in the visitor parking lot at the hospital. Staring through the windshield at the building looming before me, the unruly insects threaten to fly up my throat. I'd been in such a rush this morning to get here, but now that I've arrived, I'm nervous to go inside.

I don't know what I'm so worried about. Only, maybe I do.

Now that Jake's had some time to think about it, does he regret what he did? Getting shot to protect me? What if he does? What if—

I jump, startled, as a strange noise interrupts my thoughts. Glancing around, I try to place where the sound is coming from. Unbuckling my seatbelt, I lean over, sliding my hand under the passenger seat. My fingers curl around the forgotten burner phone, pulling it out.

My stomach flips as I look at it, the butterflies suddenly replaced by hyper circus monkeys. My palms sweat as I hurry from the vehicle, knowing I have to answer the call.

"Director Jacobson?"

"I hope that it's not too early. I know you must have had a long night."

"No, it's fine. Is everything okay?"

"I think that maybe it is."

I inhale deeply. It feels like a giant weight has been lifted from my chest.

"Really?"

"The speed at which these people work is concerning, but other than that… I don't want to get your hopes up too much, but I think we're in the clear."

"How?" I ask. "I mean, what makes you think it's over?"

"Have you seen the news this morning?"

"No."

"They're airing the story."

"Already?"

"Like I said, these people work fast. And they seem more than happy to place all the blame on Ms. Harris, since she can't refute anything that's being said about her. Apparently, she was funding the entire project herself thanks to a considerable inheritance she received."

"Wouldn't that be easy to disprove?"

"It would, unless someone has ties to the bank that was used to make all the purchases. The payments have all been traced back to a single account in her name. I'm sure that they already have the source of the initial deposit in place as well."

"But what about Gordon? What's he saying?"

"They can't find him."

I look around, searching for somewhere to sit. A lack of options makes me settle for a low brick retaining wall.

"So whoever is really behind this is just going to get away with it? Move on to do the same thing somewhere else?"

"I'm afraid so."

"And there's nothing we can do about it, is there?"

"I doubt we'd get very far even if we tried."

I squeeze the bridge of my nose, trying to make sense of it all. "You really think they're just going to forget about us?"

She sighs deeply into the phone. "I'm not sure. In the grand scheme of things, we really don't pose much of a threat to them. We can't prove anything. I'm really hoping they won't deem us worth their effort, but if you're asking if you should drop your guard? No. I wouldn't advise it."

"So that's it then."

"Well." Her tone changes, the one word enough to set my nerves on edge again. "You'll be receiving a call from me later today. An official one."

I fill my lungs, bracing for impact. I told her to file my termination papers. And I already made the decision to stay here. Still, it stings. I've worked so hard for so long at building my career. It's going to be hard to see it go.

"I'm afraid I've been forced to extend your paid leave," she says.

"What?"

"Your situation is unique. Two separate fatal encounters in the span of less than a month. I've spoken with Director Kirby, and he thinks you should undergo an additional three months of therapy before we revisit the situation."

"I don't understand."

"You'll need to speak with a therapist once a week for the next three months to continue to receive your paycheck, after which we'll all have a meeting to discuss your future with the FBI. I'm not saying you won't be welcome to return, but it might be best for you to step down and become a consultant. Like I said, Agent Knox. Congratulations."

After ending the call, I walk into the hospital in a daze, half sure I must be dreaming. At any moment, I expect to wake up and find myself lying on the floor in Butch's living room only to find that the last eighteen hours were imagined as I gasp my last breath on the ancient carpet.

But I have to believe this is real. Which means I have other worries to face right now.

I stop outside Jake's room, feeling the same way I did when I was four and he'd had his tonsils out just before his seventh birthday—scared and not knowing what to expect on the other side of the door. But once I crossed the threshold at the gentle insistence of my mother's hand against my back, everything had been okay.

I'd found Jake in bed watching TV, a dozen empty Jell-O cups that he'd charmed out of the nurses on the tray before him. I hold my breath, hoping to find something similar again. To my great relief, when I open the door and step inside, I'm not disappointed.

Jake looks toward the door expectantly, a lopsided smile breaking across his face when he sees me, his expression filled with as much hope as mine must hold. Just like he had over thirty years ago, he shifts over on the bed, the invitation clear.

And just like I had back then, I hurry across the room and climb up to curl beside him. I don't know what the future will bring. But I do know that I won't have to face it alone.

OTHER BOOKS BY SHANNON HOLLINGER

CHIEF MAGGIE RILEY SERIES:

The Girl Who Lied
Their Angel's Cry
The Shadow Girl
One Last Sigh
The Day She Died

STANDALONE PSYCHOLOGICAL THRILLERS:

Best Friends Forever
The Slumber Party
Would You Rather
Her Hiding Place

READER'S NOTE

Dear Reader,

First, a very big and most sincere THANK YOU for choosing to read DEADLY SANCTUARY, the first book in the Cassidy Knox series! If you enjoyed the book, I'd be so very grateful if you took the time to leave a review. Even just a few words can have a huge impact on helping other readers to find and choose to read it as well.

I have to confess, I had so much fun writing this book. I fell in love with Cassidy and Jake (and all the animals at the sanctuary) and can't wait for you to find out where their story goes next.

The idea for this new series came about out of impatience. My husband and I have been talking about opening an animal rescue for over a decade now. I got tired of waiting. I figured I could wait another couple of decades until we retired, or I could write about it and live my best fictional life now. And when the time came to decide where to set it, there was only one option—the Florida

Everglades.

If you've ever been, you know what I'm talking about. If you haven't, please know that it's more than just sweltering heat and giant swarms of mosquitoes (though at certain times of the year that seems hard to believe). There's something wild and dark about the landscape, a quiet beauty as serene as it is potentially deadly. In other words, it's one of my happy places. I hope that this series will make it one of yours as well.

If you'd like to keep up with my latest book news and releases, please consider following me on Amazon or BookBub. Even better, sign up for my monthly newsletter via my website (www.shannonhollinger.com) where you can enter to win signed books, find out about contests for additional prizes, make your voice heard by voting on cover designs, titles, etc., become an ARC reader, and so much more! (Your email address will never be shared, and you can unsubscribe at any time.)

Thank you so much for your support — it really is hugely appreciated!

Until next time,

Shannon Hollinger

ACKNOWLEDGEMENTS

First, I owe a huge thank you to reader Carol Nauss, winner of my tagline contest. I'm so pleased to use her words on the cover of this book! Thank you, Carol!

To beta readers Heather Flaherty (@thrillology_explorer) and Felecia Mebane (@thebookisdone), thank you both so much for being such amazing supporters and for all you do for the book community!

Thank you to proofreader Melissa Ammons and her "eagle eyes".

To my mom, Stacy. It's from her that I get my love of reading and writing… and my muscles! Thank you for all the endless trips to the library, that amazing place where they let us leave with as many books as our arms could carry, and for your endless patience while I tried my best to work my way through every book on the shelves.

To my dad, Bob, who never got to see me achieve

my dreams, but always believed I would one day. Thank you for never doubting me.

To my grandmother, Marvis. Thank you for indulging my book addiction, encouraging my sweet tooth, and for introducing me to the work of so many great authors!

To my husband, Ben. Thank you for always being up for an adventure and for our shared dream of opening our own animal sanctuary one day. And thank you for agreeing to be a "technical advisor" for this new series, though I failed to tell him that I had the gun and car details covered, and it was the romance I'd need help with—plot twist! (Cue my most devious laugh laugh.)

And mostly, a big, huge, giant THANK YOU to you, reader!

My endless gratitude goes to all of you readers, reviewers, librarians, booksellers, BookTokers, Bookstagrammers, and everyone else out there who takes the time to share your love of reading. You all deserve something special, so go ahead and get that new book you've got your eye on!
And if you care to give as well as receive, reviews make the best gift. Please consider leaving a few words for not just my books, but all those you enjoy.

ABOUT THE AUTHOR

With degrees in Crime Scene Technology and Physical Anthropology, Florida writer Shannon Hollinger hasn't just seen the dark side of humanity—she's been elbow deep inside of it! She's an avid animal lover, reader, and hiker, and has been known to use her forensic skills to figure out who ate the last cookie in the house.

A multi-genre, Amazon charts top 20 best-selling author, Shannon writes psychological thrillers filled with jaw-dropping twists and shocking endings, the police procedural Chief Maggie Riley mysteries, where the darkness of the Maine wilderness is rivaled only by the deadly secrets it conceals, and the romantic suspense Cassidy Knox mystery thrillers, where the animals will steal your heart and the nights are as hot as the days.

Her novels have been translated into multiple languages, and her short fiction has appeared in Suspense Magazine, Mystery Weekly, and The Saturday Evening Post, among many other magazines and anthologies.

Shannon is a member of the International Thriller Writers and the Short Mystery Fiction Society.

To keep current on book news and to enter monthly giveaways, sign up for Shannon's newsletter through her website, www.shannonhollinger.com.

Find Shannon on social media:

Facebook @thiswritersays
Instagram @thiswritersays
BookBub @shannonhollinger
TikTok   @shannonhollinger
Pinterest @thiswritersays